YO-DJO-224

152.4
Gel
C.1   89-17008

51498

(dup. card)

AUTHOR

Gelinas, Paul J.

TITLE

Coping With Anger   (Revised)

DATE DUE	BORROWER'S NAME	ROOM NUMBER
OCT 4 — 1991	Ericka M Sanchez	215
OCT 1 0 1991	Rebecca Nadasky	315
DEC 6 1991	Cary Lehman	42
OCT 2 ? '92	Valerie A ...	

DATE
JAN

51498   89-17008

152.4
Gel
C.1

Gelinas, Paul J.
Coping with Anger. -
Revised edition

Lourdes High School Library
4034 West 56th Street
Chicago, Illinois 60629

COPING WITH ANGER

PAUL J. GELINAS

THE ROSEN PUBLISHING GROUP, Inc.
New York

Lourdes High School Library
4034 West 56th Street
Chicago, Illinois 60629

Published in 1979, 1981, 1983, 1988 by The Rosen Publishing Group, Inc.
29 East 21st Street, New York, N.Y. 10010

Copyright 1979, 1988 by Paul J. Gelinas 89 - 17008

All rights reserved. No part of this book may be
reproduced in any form without written permission
from the publisher, except by a reviewer.

Revised Edition 1988

Library of Congress Cataloging in Publication Data
Gelinas, Paul J.
  Coping with anger.

  Includes index
  (Personal guidance/social adjustment series)
  1. Anger. I. Title.
BF575.A5G44   152.4   78-18928
ISBN 0-8239-0780-5

51498

Manufactured in the United States of America

152.4
GEL
c.1

About the Author

PAUL J. GELINAS is a clinical psychologist in private practice and a lecturer at the University of the State of New York at Stony Brook. He is a former teacher and superintendent of schools. His educational degrees include the B.A., M.A., M.Sc. and Ed.D.

He is the author of twelve books, two of which were selected as bonus books by the Book-of-the-Month Club.

Among his professional affiliations, he is a member of the Suffolk County Psychological Association and the Council for the Advancement of the Psychological Professions and Sciences. He is listed in such publications as the *National Register of Health Services in Psychology, National Register of Educational Researchers, Contemporary Authors,* the *World Who's Who of Authors,* and the *Dictionary of International Biography.*

His civic activities include positions on the Three Village Board of Education and the Civic Association of the Setaukets, and he is a former president of the Lions Club of Setauket.

As special recognition of his contributions to community leadership, the Paul J. Gelinas Junior High School in Setauket, New York, was named for him.

Contents

CHAPTER I

Are You Angry?

Suzanne tried in vain not to think of the problem that had been festering in her mind for many days. She slammed down her history workbook and turned on her small radio, filling the room with the blare of hard rock.

Sitting cross-legged on the pink bedspread, she vacillated between sadness and rebellion. Her lithe body swayed and jerked to the mesmerizing rhythm. She visualized Bill, loose-jointed, cocky, smiling a devil-may-care challenge as though telling the world to go to hell. She could see him, sloppily dressed, high-topped sneakers, brass-buckled belt holding up his jeans. Bill was a fun guy who did not give a damn for teachers or wimps. A fellow student, dark-haired Marie, had said that he could put his shoes under her bed anytime, laughing as she dared others less cool.

Suzanne recalled the last school dance. She had endured Freddie's awkward steps while wondering why a guy like Bill never asked her to dance. After detaching herself from good old Freddie, she loitered outside, dreamy and weary.

Coarse laughter erupted from behind a clump of bushes. The spangling light of a gym window revealed a group of guys and girls sprawled on the grass. As Suzanne approached, drawn by curiosity, someone called: "Be a good sport, Suzanne. Here, have a swig of my beer." A whiff of marijuanna crossed her nostrils, a scent that both repelled her and stirred a desire she would not admit.

Now in her bedroom, she pondered: I really wanted to join them. Why did I run away? Haven't I the right to have fun like the others? Why can't I be like them? Why can't I be carefree instead of locked up in what others think—others like Mom and Dad?

Thinking of her parents, she switched off the radio, reached for her teddy bear, hugged it. She pictured her father and mother laughing together. Suzanne tried to smile, and suddenly she knew that she loved them.

Would it be Bill and Marie—or Mom and Dad? By yielding to the

fast crowd, she would somehow betray her parents. By not going with
the tide, she would deny her secret yearnings. Frustrated by ambivalence, she pounded a pillow with clenched fists.

Anger is reflected in a series of alarming statistics concerning teenagers. In a recent year a million ran away from home and 25 percent
dropped out of school. More than a million teenage girls became
pregnant, and thousands of teenagers committed suicide.

Rage is a condition of life in parts of some cities. It permeates the
rubble-strewn streets and the unheated tenements. It smolders in the
brooding faces of mothers huddled on predawn lines at welfare centers.
In clinics, many wait an entire day to see a doctor. The rage also erupts
in mindless violence. The bill for vandalism in the nation's schools is
over $600 million a year. According to a report of the National Insti-
tute of Education, during one month in American schools 282,000
students were physically attacked, 112,000 were robbed by force or
threat, and 2.4 million were victims of property theft. The report also
noted the "rising tide of drugs, weapons, and disorderly conduct."

Teachers say that violence follows a pattern set by television programs shown the previous week. The typical high school graduate has
spent 15,000 hours watching TV—4,000 hours more than he has spent
in school. He has witnessed 18,000 murders and innumerable beatings,
shootings, car wrecks, robberies, and bombings.

Teenagers indeed are not without their own teachers in the arts of
violence. Titles such as these are found on bookstore shelves: *How To
Kill... The Death Dealer's Manual... The Perfect Crime and How to
Commit It....Duty Free Smuggling Made Easy.*

Abusive parents flail out at their children with belts, broomsticks,
shoes, even electric cords. About 10 percent are burned by matches,
electric irons, cigarette butts, or hot radiators. Almost ten million
parents use a gun or knife on their children, and 2,000 battered kids die
each year from such assaults, as reported by the National Center of
Child Abuse.

It is a common assumption that parents who wreak violence and
anger on their children are poor, uneducated, or disadvantaged.
Research shows, however, that abusive parents are found in all socio-
economic, racial, and religious groups.

Many wives cannot escape violence even in their home. Mary's husband, for example, a construction foreman, beat her several times in
their eighteen months of marriage. Once he choked her until she felt

she was about to die. Finally, when he threatened to harm their baby, she knew that the marriage must end. An estimate based on police and family court records points to one million women who yearly are battered by husband or boyfriend.

Many teenagers bear the baneful effects of violence in the home. The anger, as though absorbed by osmosis, reappears in later years and they in turn inflict violence and uncontrolled anger on their own mate and children.

A casual date can turn into violence. For Debbie it seemed harmless and fun when a classmate pulled over to the curb and invited her to get in. "We'll just cruise around a bit," he said.

Hesitating a moment, Debbie nevertheless slid into the front seat. He laughed the laugh of a guy sure of himself.

"I often see you in school," she began. "You're a senior and popular. Why should you pay attention to me?"

"I noticed you all right," he replied. "The way you walk is real sexy."

"Oh," she said, then added, "This is a snazy car."

"Real cool," he emphasized. A grin twisted his lips. She closed her eyes listening to the radio as the car weaved in and out of traffic. Debbie felt happy, glad that this good-looking fellow had chosen her. But on the outskirts of town she grew a little apprehensive. "Where are we going?" she asked.

"Here," he said, heading into a side road, then turning sharply on an unpaved stretch. Finally the car stopped, and darkness took over.

"Please turn on the lights—it's too spooky."

Instead, he reached for her, pulled her to his body.

"Let's get out of here," she said, struggling against his pawing hands.

"Why?" he asked. "A little petting is no harm. And you're not a virgin, I bet."

She pushed hard against him. "Please—please get me away from this God-forsaken place." Breathless, she added, "I've never done this before."

Hours later, dazed and hardly conscious of her surroundings at home, she groped on tiptoes toward her bedroom. "I'm okay," she answered her mother's sleepy enquiry from the adjacent room. But she wasn't okay. Looking in the mirror, she recoiled. Her face was bruised, her underthings were torn, her hair was disheveled and hanging loosely as though in total defeat. In the shower, she tortured herself with water as hot as she could stand. Her whole being seemed irrevocably soiled, utterly vile and repulsive. That first experience should have been an act of love, she told herself. Instead it had been brutal. She had been robbed of something that could never be replaced. Only the shame and the anger remained.

Many teenagers have been desensitized to violence. Too often they have identified with characters who push women around as if they were mere objects to exploit. But why would a person, no matter how alienated, attack uprotected old folks, not only robbing them but sometimes inflicting unimaginable cruelty? Why does a mugger feel impelled to beat a victim even when no resistance is offered? Why is the human being so frequently the most vicious of animals? Incidentally, it has been observed by psychologists that the hater of gays carries within himself the subconscious fear of his own homosexuality.

The macho image purveyed by the mass media is often assumed by teenagers to hide their insecurity with the opposite sex. This phony self-image can lead to the ultimate degradation of women: rape.

It is known, of course, that rape is not motivated by sexual needs. Rather the perpetrator is impelled by the desire to dominate and to humiliate his victim. It should also be noted that two thirds of reported rapes are committed by persons know to the victim: a boyfriend, neighbor, or family friend. About half of the 70,000 rapes reported annually are acquaintance rapes.

There are other sexual dilemmas for teenagers. Mary Anne, for example, a sixteen-year-old student, discovered that she was pregnant. She had assumed that one cannot be impregnated the first time of sexual intercourse.

Jimmy, her boyfriend, had not appeared worried. "Damn it," he said. "I thought you could take care of yourself."

"Care for myself?" she flung back. "I didn't do this by myself."

Jostled by the rush of students in the hall, she felt cold and rejected, aware that he was more embarrassed than worried. "You said you loved me," she whispered as though to herself. The bell rang for the next class.

"I'll see you tomorrow—okay?"

"Okay," she replied, holding back the tears.

Still she had an irresistible urge to have the baby. Late at night she tossed sleepless, contemplating one plan after another. She could have the child, she thought, and give it up for adoption. but as long as I live—well, it would be my flesh and blood; I'd always wonder what happened to him or her.

Irene, a trusted friend, had been married for two years. Mary Anne sought her advice, noting her ten-month-old infant. "He's so cute," she said. "I'd love my baby, too."

Irene took off her little apron. "Sit down," she said, pointing to the kitchen table. "You think a baby is a little doll. But are you ready to face the world without a husband to support you while you go through the pain of pregnancy?"

"The pain?" Mary Anne questioned.

"The morning sickness," Irene began, "constipation, water retention, weight gain, backache, leg aches, nausea, pelvic pain. And you'll be angry because you'll be alone. That's having a baby," Irene concluded, then added, "Are you ready for that?"

"What shall I do?" Mary Anne wailed. "Mother wants me to get married. But Jimmy wouldn't want that, nor me."

Irene left the table and her teacup and walked slowly toward the sink, saying under her breath, "I had an abortion before I was married."

"An abortion?" Mary Anne threw up her hands. "My mother would kill me. It would be murder in her eyes."

But for many days Mary Anne haunted the library, reading everything she could find on the subject.

She learned that three techniques are used in abortion. The technique most often employed in early pregnancy is the D & C, or *dilation* and *curettage*. The uterus is reached through the vagina, the cervix having been stretched by using a curette, a small hoelike instrument. The doctor then scrapes the wall of the uterus. Bleeding is considerable.

Another method is *suction abortion*. A suction tube is inserted through the dilated cervix into the uterus. More than two thirds of the abortions performed in the United States and Canada employ this procedure.

When pregnancy is more advanced, risking too much bleeding by the D & C or suction techniques, doctors use the *saline abortion*. This method is used after sixteen weeks of pregnancy when enough amniotic fluid has gathered in the sac around the baby. A long needle is pushed through the mother's abdomen. Concentrated salt is absorbed through the lungs and the gastrointestinal tract. The mother, having submitted to the operation for about an hour, generally goes into labor the next day and delivers a dead baby.

A Gallup poll reveals that 52 percent of young people between 13 and 19 are sexually active. The National Governors' Association reports that in that age group approximately one million pregnancies occur each year.

Martha, a sixteen-year-old high school student, had suffered what appeared to be too much deprivation to fight off a drastic end to her young life. Illegitimate, she had never seen nor heard anything good about her father. The only link with him was an Ingersoll watch that her mother had thrown in the wastepaper basket, saying, "It's no good—just like its owner." Surreptitiously, Martha had retrieved the watch and treasured it through the years.

Martha was left with her grandparents while her mother worked as a waitress in another town, visiting her only occasionally. She lived her first eight years with the old people, who were free in blaming her for her mother's indiscretion. The acid temper of her guardians gradually engendered resentment in Martha so that she was considered unruly and emotionally unstable. Yet there was a richness in her soul that she felt whenever she fondled the old watch in secret. Along with it was bitterness stirred by loneliness and disappointment. She cherished love for her lost father and held a smoldering hatred of her mother for having abandoned her.

One evening as Martha washed and dried dishes, her grandmother sat rigid in her chair, knitting and darting an occasional glance of disapproval toward the child. Nervous, Martha dropped a dish. It shattered on the floor. She awaited the old lady's tirade of fury.

"You're no good for anything!" The woman turned to her husband. "This little one is evil, the product of a vile sin."

Martha crept up the narrow stairs to her room in the attic. She wanted to die. Muffling her cries against the pillow, she wondered if she really was an ugly creature spewed out of her mother's womb. Suddenly she thought that her father could be standing there to claim her as his own.

Days later her mother appeared, driving her own car. "Your grandparents don't want you anymore." Then she added, "It's all right: I meant to have you with me anyway—I'm married now."

Later, Martha held her mother's hand, dragging her ragged suitcase. At last they had arrived at a ranch house on Long Island. It seemed like a palace, with carpeted living room, kitchen shining with white appliances.

The years passed. Yet Martha's home life continued to be turbulent, with frequent quarrels between her mother and Mike, her stepfather. And withal there was always Martha's fear of being abandoned again.

Her school progress, however, had been good. She expected to be graduated from high school in the current year.

Meanwhile, her yearning for affection led her to encourage the advances of a young teacher who was serving his internship for state certification. Then came a devastating blow.

After Mike left for work one morning, her mother sipped coffee, nervously dragging on a cigarette. Martha assumed that the woman's icy demeanor was a mere residue of another marital quarrel, but her mother stood up, balancing herself unsteadily. "You little bastard," she blurted. "I know all about you and Mike—he told me." She folded her arms rigidly across her bosom. "How could you? You've caused me too much trouble—God, I wish you had never been born."

"But . . . " Martha's lower lip trembled. She could not speak, nor point out that her stepfather had threatened to throw her out of the house if she did not yield.

Her mother paced the floor. She pointed a quivering finger. "You're graduating in two weeks," she said. "After that you're out of here—I never want to see your face again, never."

The following days were black with despair. Again Martha was abandoned. But perhaps there was one hope: Stanley, the teacher who had made love with her. Surely he would understand. She would cry, and he would hold her as if he were her lost father.

But when she ventured to his apartment he was not interested in her tears. He merely wanted her in bed, and he warned that she must never reveal their affair. With a little cry like that of a stricken animal, she felt that the world was indeed rotten—with no one to love her.

On graduation night she sat with hundreds of others, the stage brightly illuminated. Strangely she seemed enveloped in an unearthly radiance. People who knew her were puzzled by her transformation.

Since her parents had not attended the ceremony, a teacher drove her home. She carried an armful of flowers available to any graduate who wished to take them from the empty stage. Without a word she went to her room and closed the door. She arranged the flowers like a bower on the bed and lay down, clutching her father's watch.

She had planned well to take her own life. To paraphrase Schopenhauer, the terror of her life outweighed the terror of death.

A suicide occurs in the United States every 19 minutes. Among these are 5,000 adolescents annually, with an added 250,000 who fail in the attempt. Suicide is the third leading cause of death among teenagers. In addition, about 15 percent of auto deaths should be classified as suicide, according to researchers Alex D. Pokorny and James D. Smith of Baylor College of Medicine.

Surprisingly, few poor children kill themselves. Within a four-year period, however, more than forty young people took their lives in a cluster of towns north of Chicago, one of the wealthiest suburban areas in the country.

Heavy pressures are imposed on teenagers in our competitive and changing society. Unwise parents and others often fail to meet the criteria of common sense and decency. It is little wonder that an increasing number of young people seem to be disturbed emotionally.

A case in point was that of Ted, the only son of a school principal. From an early age the boy had been pressured with the necessity of making a good impression in the community to reflect the civic importance of his father.

Unfortunately, from being a bright pupil in elementary school Ted had slipped into mediocrity in junior high and finally into failure in senior high. Now he was deemed unqualified for graduation. His parents, acutely conscious of their social prestige, felt disgraced. The young man seemed to be repaying his proud parents with anger and ingratitude.

And yet an impartial observer might have questioned who was the most emotionally perverted: the parents with their false values or the inscrutable Ted? The school principal and his social-climbing wife were more concerned with outward appearances than with real affection for their son. The man preached respect for children in public, then conveyed little kindness at home.

The only weapon possessed by some teenagers against their elders is to run counter to their scale of values. Unfortunately this anger becomes a corrosive poison in the personality of many young people. It leaves them weakened in their struggle for healthful adjustment, their search for a self-image that can sustain them in times of stress.

This school administrator had at his command a host of helpers for his son: school psychologist, guidance personnel, vocational specialist, school nurse, social workers, special tutors—each with his symbolic pill of cure. If only he had realized that this host of professionals had meager influence without one simple remedy that had all along been readily available—simple love honestly prescribed without deception and phoniness.

Anger and violence seems to be graffiti scrawled in the hearts of people by an evil force. But it would be a mistake to assume that anger, which appears to be innate in all of us—must be associated always with evil. Anger is as often used constructively as destructively. Just as electricity can kill, that very same source of energy can keep you warm, cook your food, and in fact help to meet your needs for a happier existence. By the same token, in order to control your anger, you must understand its nature, learn how to direct it toward constructive ends. Thus you can make it a useful tool for greater understanding and a better life.

CHAPTER II

The Nature of Our Anger

What makes us act like vicious animals against our fellowmen and against ourselves?

What is the origin of anger and its extreme form called hate?

John Dollard and Associates and many other researchers in the field of human conduct have concluded that "aggression is always the consequence of frustration." More specifically, scientists assert that the occurrence of aggressive behavior always presupposes the existence of frustration. More simply stated, whenever we feel blocked in getting what we really desire and need for our well-being, our survival, we tend to become angry and are inclined to fight for our right to exist. From daily observation, it seems reasonable to recognize that aggressive behavior is always traceable to some form of denial in meeting our needs.

Children who feel slighted and neglected, for example, often become experts in annoying parents, teachers, and other authorities. Those who are downtrodden by the monotony of their environment turn upon helpless minorities to persecute and to hurt. Mobs, too long frustrated by injustice, lack of opportunities, poverty, and discrimination, take on a grimness and cruelty not expected of people ordinarily gentle and kind. Finally, nations long hindered from realizing their rightful aspirations, denied and beset by suspicion, will make war upon each other with Vandalic lack of humanity.

In short, whenever you can be expected to perform certain acts for your welfare, and these acts are prevented from occurring, the result is always the arousal of some degree of anger, either withheld or expressed.

Frustration is therefore the condition in a person that exists when he fails to reach or is prevented from reaching a given goal. *Aggression* is the urge to act; it is also action itself aimed toward the removal of frustration. If justified and normal aggression is continuously prevented from expression, the consequence is always a greater urge to find an outlet, a building up to a greater intensity that finally can turn into hate, the impulse to act ruthlessly with bitterness toward the environment or the self. Hatred is therefore an ever potential factor, inherent or acquired, that emerges when aggression is too long denied.

Acts of violence are the most obvious forms of overaggression. Calculated plans for vengeance also are silently evolved in fantasies of brutal attacks by an aggrieved person. Actual and overt forays with questionable business deals, malicious rumors, and even a mocking grin may be part of the armament of hatred, including, as already noted, the masochism of drug addiction and suicide.

We are now concerned with further clarification of what is technically called the *frustration-aggression hypothesis* as defined by numerous scientists. Sigmund Freud, for instance, worked systematically and extensively with the formula, also stating that frustration —being denied what one needs—inevitably results in aggression. This aggression may be directly expressed or be repressed, later perhaps to seek expression in irrational behavior and self-defeating neurosis.

William James said that man when subject to severe frustration is the most ruthless and ferocious of all beasts. William McDougall spoke of the same phenomenon as the "instinct of combat," and he reemphasized that this instinct is aroused by "obstructions."

This combative behavior is present in the whole animal kingdom. It can, at times, have no specific objects, becoming a generalized reaction to overall inadequate conditions.

The frustration-aggression hypothesis simply states that if our needs are not met, we become frustrated and then angry. This concept therefore tends to explain broad and puzzling present-day problems, such as murders, race prejudice, sibling jealousy, riots, arson, gang fights, wife beating, and child abuse, not to mention the morbid popularity of violence in detective stories, the fascination aroused by the lurid, the cruelty depicted so vividly in movies and on television.

Lack of understanding concerning anger and hate has allowed these emotions to run rampant. Uncontrolled hate—the extreme form of anger—is a virulence which if not drained by a new approach must soon crush us all.

Hate seems to be an inevitable concomitant of our culture and mores. It impels any animal, including man, to thrash about, to fight, and to turn aggressively against obstacles that stand in the way of satisfying needs.

Heredity has endowed us with two basic instincts, according to Freud, one to love, the other to hate—one that is constructive and the other destructive. *Eros* is the drive to live and *Thanatos* the urge to die. We come into the world grasping for life but also with the innate inevitability of death. Our existence itself must be a process ultimately leading to oblivion. But before the final defeat, the flow leading thereto can be used in the service of a richer and more abundant life. But before reaching that goal, we must grapple with our baser nature, become familiar with its devious expression of hate, and learn how to control it.

Just as love in psychological literature is frequently defined as a wide spectrum from mere attraction to an intense desire for an object, so hate or its genesis is herein described as a dislike to the other extreme of wishing to destroy. The degree of hate will tend to vary in intensity and depth in proportion to the extent of frustration that aroused it.

This variation may be conveyed by different words to replace the term hate, such as overaggression, annoyance, irritation, exasperation, hostility, and maliciousness. The motives and aims of hate range from wishing to destroy, to cause damage, to torment, to retaliate, to humiliate, threaten, insult—and also, paradoxically, the desire to destroy in order to rebuild on a firmer foundation. Terrorists and other activists, of course, seek to justify their attacks against defenseless people by this last motive.

In terms of psychological dynamics, and also for convenience in our discussion, it might be well to distinguish five kinds of hate: (1) incipient; (2) inward; (3) explosive; (4) deflected; and (5) constructive.

Incipient hate is an initial aversion or dislike that impels one to action against the frustration that has caused it. That kind of anger is like precancerous cells on the verge of spreading into real malignancy. This mild form of potential hate is comparatively easy to neutralize or at least to prevent from developing into a vicious emotion if steps are taken early to remove some obstacle.

You may, for example, be introduced to a person whose seemingly haughty manner arouses a spontaneous dislike. "I could easily hate that person," you may say. It is possible that the initial antagonism could become malicious because the person appears to be a threat to your sense of security and a potential frustration to your self-expression.

Yet after questioning a mutual acquaintance, you may find out that the person whom you could so easily learn to detest is, after all, a very shy person whose manner actually reflects a fear of meeting strangers. Accordingly, later you discover that he is quite a charming and kind man. The threatened frustration has thus been removed, and the original dislike, instead of progressing to hostility, is replaced by a warm and friendly feeling. Even when there is some solid basis for dislike, hate can be arrested in its course by overt and comparatively mild disapproval—if expressed immediately. This type of incipient hate, however, can be the more easily handled if in the home a child has been regularly allowed to show anger in harmless venting of each small squall soon to be dissipated without fuss or retaliation.

Inward hate is also aroused by frustration, but it is then turned inward because of fear that the expression of anger will bring unbearable reprisals from the outside world.

Hate that is repressed from consciousness, however, is not thereby eliminated but continues to operate within the person, venting its nature against the self, corroding the psyche, and leading frequently to mental aberration and numerous other disorders and anxieties.

A girl, for example, was employed in a store where the boss was a harsh woman, the prototype of the severe, unfeeling, and punitive parent. The young girl, unable to obtain other employment, which she sorely needed, continued under difficult circumstances, abusive threats, and inadequate facilities. Still she repressed out of fear the anger that the situation warranted.

She never complained, she smiled her martyr's smile, carried her burden without a murmur, apparently with no resentment of any sort. Yet she was almost constantly afflicted with headaches and vague pains. Finally, with added discord at home, she became disoriented, baffled by inability to concentrate, bothered by compulsive thoughts; and at last her condition deteriorated into what her physician diagnosed as a nervous breakdown.

Explosive hate bursts forth generally without warning. This kind of hate is unreasonable, blind, venting its fury indiscriminately upon the environment as if a dam had suddenly given way and the rushing water of long-hidden hostility now engulfed all in its path.

Hate, therefore, that is turned inward continues to build up tension. If too long denied, it may lead to uncontrolled and irrational behavior and other antisocial acts including riots, mass murders, senseless destruction, wars, and revolutions.

Mary, nineteen years old, was a tragic example. She had devoted years as the sole support and caretaker of her widowed mother. The older and nagging woman had been confined to a wheelchair for three years. Mary nevertheless professed a deep and undying love for her mother. In fact, she had deprived herself of male companionship, thoughts of marriage, and even of dating, denying herself a life of her own. She toiled away at what she considered and willingly accepted as her duty. She was indeed loyal, and people commented on her endless patience and kindness.

The day came when something broke within her. Neighbors were suddenly mystified to hear that this gentle and docile girl had hurled herself upon her mother in an explosive burst of unexplained destructiveness. Disheveled and clawing as she was led out by the police, she screamed, "I didn't want to hurt her. I don't know why. God, how I loved my mother!"

She had been robbed of her teenage years and of her rightful destiny during the period of life when within her pulsed a desire for self-expression, for the realization of repressed dreams. The frustration and unacknowledged hostility seemed destined ultimately to find some irrational and awful consequences. "Wherever we look in the animal kingdom," wrote McDougall, "the same rule seems to obtain: in general terms, the stronger the impulse at work in an animal, the more readily is the combative behavior evoked by any obstruction from other creatures, if the species is at all capable of response."

Deflected hate is displaced from one object to another, thus allowing expression without hurting the original object. Just as love can be transferred from one person to another, so hate can be shifted. The chances are excellent in the average person that if he be disappointed or rejected by a potential mate, his affection will ultimately be attached to someone else. Irritation, likewise, may be projected on anyone handy if the original object is not available or suitable for its wrathful reception.

Jimmy, who looked much older than his age, had married soon after high school graduation. He found himself promoted to floor walker in a fashionable retail outlet, and people considered him lucky indeed. He was compelled to be gracious and polite at all times while on the job. The customer was always right. Jimmy received the generally wealthy and demanding clientele with an ever-ready smile, always responding with congenial restraint even when unnecessarily rebuked and abused. The day-after-day annoyances were nerve-wracking and too frequently unreasonable. The salary, on the other hand, was good, and chances for advancement were excellent.

With wry humor, Jimmy explained how he deflected his hostility against inanimate objects instead of aiming it directly at customers and employer. He gathered old furniture, worthless junk, and assorted pieces, which he stored in his attic. When he came home at night, particularly after a trying day, he proceeded immediately to the attic and there in a frenzy of delightful destruction, he broke up furniture, cursed loud and clear, and aimed chairs at imagined customers. And then free at last from the restraints his job imposed upon him, he slowly descended the stairs and kissed his wife, both genuinely smiling now and happy because they understood.

In many years as a clinical psychologist working with young adults, I cannot recall a single case of neurosis or emotional disturbance that did not have unresolved anger as the main overt or intrinsic element in the disorder.

The common sequence in the progress of serious emotional problems nearly always follows the same course. First, there have been repeated and continuing frustrations, generally pervading the child's experiences. Whether early or late, frustrations appeared persistently in family life, in love, in physical illness, in work or play, hounding the person until at last he was incapable of withstanding further hindrances to personal expression and self-realization.

In such circumstances, if the mechanism of adjustment does not work, the first complex of frustration inevitably calls forth a second step. The person becomes angry, even though he may not acknowledge that hostility. When the anger has chronically invaded his being, the emotionally sick person does one of two things: he either strikes out against people and objects in his environment, or he holds back the anger, refusing to admit its existence, actually turning it against himself.

The person may deflect his bitterness into channels such as failing in school or college as a subconscious desire to strike back at his parents or other authority figures. On the other hand, the person may excel in a spiteful effort to show that he is better than anyone else. A lawyer, for example, with that chronic state of mind may attain great wealth, ruthlessly fighting any authority figure as if that opponent were a symbol of his own parent or parents who had so frustrated him in childhood.

The more pitiable is the person who blames himself, who grows up faulting himself for inadequacy and inferiority. He may say to himself that it was not his upbringing that was wholly or partially responsible; rather, he was solely at fault. If he had been stronger, more attractive, smarter, he would now not feel so frustrated and insignificant.

Regardless of whether a person vents his anger against society in self-defeating ways or against himself, there is always a sense of guilt as a third step. This guilt is very real even when others are blamed; ultimately the guilt appears in the form of taking onto himself the onus for failures. If only he had planned differently, if only he had taken greater care in executing a robbery. Guilt in various forms, aware or unaware, always touches the person whose anger is projected in a socially unacceptable manner or is turned primarily against the self.

The fourth step in the deterioration of emotional stability in an otherwise healthy person is the emergence of depression. These feelings of despair are at times very serious. Even suicide becomes possible in many young people as well as in their elders. It is a debilitating feeling, an emptiness, with little hope or sunshine to brighten existence.

A case in point was a young woman, Marie, in her first year at college. She had returned home, unable to continue her studies. Seized by one attack of discouragement after another, she was under great stress. She even sought to drive away her misery by making a feeble attempt at suicide—which was indeed a cry for help. First she complained of having no friends, no love affairs, with only an occasional date during which she felt extremely uncomfortable and unspontaneous. She felt ugly and unattractive. Yet in fact she was a very pretty girl, with a good figure and an allure that should have made her a desirable companion.

Her family was upper middle class—a doting father and an oversolicitous mother. As long as Marie—who came into my office accompanied by her mother—remained at home before going to college, she had functioned well, with some friends and apparent good adjustment. It was only after she had left home that her personality problem arose. Early in her teens she had been warned emphatically, again and again, of disasters that could come from sexual contacts.

Fundamentally of a sensual nature, well-endowed and sensitive, with sudden desires in college, she was caught in a net of frustration. To keep the love of her parents, she had to be chaste and a virgin. To deny herself sexual satisfaction, she had to withdraw from dates and the free-swinging ways of many of her colleagues.

Apart from the conflicts thus revealed, she withheld from her consciousness anger against her parents for creating this dilemma in her life. It took some time before she would accept this anger as somewhat justified. Her attempt at suicide, in fact, had its basis in her need to punish her parents. She visualized with great sadness her parents' sorrow and guilt as they gazed upon her virginal and dead body.

Gradually came a better understanding of the conflicts with which her psyche had struggled, together with the anger and the resultant guilt and depression. Finally she was relieved of her melancholy and the sense of emptiness.

Most psychologists working with disturbed people now know of this sequence, acknowledging the pain and anger that unmet needs evoke in those who do not recognize the function of frustration in mental disturbances.

CHAPTER III

Some Constructive Avenues

We have investigated unacceptable and harmful aggressions. If these were the only kinds of anger, our civilization would certainly have consumed itself into oblivion and chaos. Fortunately there exists in the human psyche a drive for the positive expression of aggressive behavior, serving both the individual and society as a whole.

Constructive hate is indeed a positive force. Hate, like fire, which is inevitable in our culture, can be controlled for human welfare. It can certainly be consciously directed into sociably acceptable channels. In the process an individual can be cleansed of his own insidious hate, leaving him free for dignity and self-possession. The art of hating, paradoxically, can thus emancipate a person for a healthier mental life. It can satisfy his hunger for release of tensions, and without the hindrance of neurotic obstacles at last leave him free to love.

There are many injustices to hate, to fight against. There are poverty, unjust wars, the endless frustrations that hinder salvation. Challenges abound for everyone to become involved in the solution of vexing problems. There are countless doors to ventilate our hatred, to aggrandize mankind, and to reach out for happiness. As Christ drove out the money changers from the temple, so one has many outlets for constructive hate, for good rather than for negativism.

Hate, however, seems almost always to have been considered a secondary phenomenon, an absence of love, rather than as an entity with its own powerful dynamics. Our task is therefore to accept as a reality the inevitability of hate, and then to handle that hostility in a practical and effective manner.

The repressive forces in the individual, as pointed out by Wilhelm Reich, usually combine with those of our culture to keep most citizens tied to conventional norms of a society that seeks comparative stability. A conformist, for example, was considered a good subject of kings or rulers. By repressing individual anger, classes and the establishment were quite safe—until explosive inner hatred finally burst its bounds in terrible times of war and revolution.

The reckoning was periodic and frequently governed by those in power, who determined when a man should kill his neighbor. Thus at a convenient time was the demon of hatred released that had so long been held tightly within the inner parts of the mind. Before such release of his repression of anger, man was effectively and patriotically enslaved in own status quo, his mortgages, the threat of hunger, of insecurity, and of the ever-present guilt in his religion, which damned him to eternal torments in the hereafter if he did not adhere to the dictates of his superiors and of society.

Man, according to this view, endured the sufferings of inward hate, imprisoned within himself because he feared a greater punishment from without, from an intangible mesh that others had in large part intertwined with individual neurosis to control him. The theory of class struggle, according to Marxian doctrine and the state itself, depends by implication on the frustration-aggression principle described.

Past generations could easily be mobilized for warfare. For the majority of people it was only at such times of national crisis that their primitive instincts were allowed free rein without guilt. Thus the opportunity for direct expression of hate tended to make it unnecessary to justify war. The state of emergency was a sudden and highly satisfactory way of breaking free from the mores of a civilization that had hitherto succeeded in imposing its institutions and repressions. People poured into the streets, exuberant in their ignorance, waving flags in the face of death.

There are, of course, many other defenses against hate in order to divert it from oneself. Aggression can be displaced or sublimated. We may also project upon others the traits that we dislike in ourselves. Detesting his weakness, a man may through self-deception ascribe those weaknesses to others, as if saying that it is not he who is full of hatred; it is his neighbor who hates him. Through the defensive device of reaction formation, we might even persuade ourselves that we love our enemies. This is so much easier than to admit animosity toward them—and safer, too. Charles Brenner wrote, in *An Elementary Textbook of Psychoanalysis,* "This seems to be particularly true if the object or person in question is powerful, a type of identification with the aggressor." Perhaps in this mechanism lies the power of all dictators.

Obviously there are better ways to handle one's hostility than the self-defeating behavior discussed above. Bottled-up aggressions are positively released in sports. "After work," Karl Menninger said, "play is the most universal method of safely disposing of our aggression." An opponent becomes a substitute for the original object of our hate, even in vicarious satisfaction when we are mere spectators. Epithets are flung at the referee, curses are hurled at the opposing team—all in good fun, although the hatred thus disposed of is real enough.

Much of our play and recreation partake of outlets for unacceptable aggression. Children play with war toys, enjoy violent movies with guns, planes, projectiles, and brutality—all means of releasing negative emotions born of frustrations. Even pornography may serve as a safety valve for guilt-ridden aggression in frustrated sex and unrequited physical love. Promiscuity itself may be deflected hatred within the confines of subconscious conflicts and fears. Controversial as some of these devices may be, the fact remains that the dynamics of the frustration-aggression hypothesis are involved.

A person may advantageously sublimate sadism perhaps by becoming a surgeon or a policeman. Lack of love and other deprivations may find some compensation in the arts and sciences, in business, in work. But it must be admitted that some of these indirect ways of giving vent to our hates are at times self-defeating, as evidenced in the case of a person who jumped from his hotel window at a time that appeared to be his greatest business triumph. Man's ultimate salvation nevertheless must be sought in confrontation with his environment by directing his hates toward definite objectives, by committing himself to hate things that are detrimental to himself and to his fellowmen. One must be committed and allow his being to merge in movements greater than himself, canalize his hatred against evil instead of permitting it to corrode his inner self.

Although violence is obviously not uncommon among us, still a relatively small group have in desperation chosen that route for the release of their tensions. The vast majority have not espoused this direct expression of explosive and blind hate in a frantic reaching out for emancipation, nor have they sensed the wisdom of channeling their hates constructively. They are the withdrawing and submissive ones, the silent majority, either finding some meager degree of expressing their hates, or repressing them to lie there as the foundation for possible character disorders—having endured their frustrations too long in quiet desperation. They still dodge the confrontation, living with their neuroses, hugging tight in intimate masochism, vainly hoping for deliverance in some mysterious way either in this life or thereafter.

And yet an acceptance of reality, a fearless confrontation of things as they are, reveals that hate is indeed a double-edged sword that can cut to the right as well as to the left—to destruction and even to the ultimate annihilation of man. Nevertheless, hate can be the main instrument of his struggle against a hostile environment. To say that our culture is largely the product of neurotic drives may be shocking and yet not so tragic as it would appear. To hint that the vast technological and scientific progress partakes of a compulsive urge to strike out, to lay about, and to create as well as to change the world is indeed to say that our discomfort and man's attempt to improve his lot comprise an escape from pain, a race against madness—as Vincent Van Gogh had to create in order to maintain his sanity, to paint, ever to paint in his struggle to survive against the torments within him.

Music and other forms of art are, of course, a sublimation of unrealized hopes and dreams. The music of yesteryear was generally subdued and soft, symbolizing a tendency to subservience. Today popular music has become harsh, strident, with a wild rhythm, a syncopation of sounds rebellious as a reflection of inner pulsation, always on the verge of spilling over, unrestrained and aggressive. Our dance has returned to the primitive, a spasmodic twitching, projecting a muscular language of pugnacious yearnings.

But art is said to be a hatred of ugliness and disharmony. Science is hate of disorder and lack of order. Honesty is the dislike of dishonesty, and justice is the abhorrence of injustice.

As bold confrontation in the past invoked great and sometimes disturbing changes in government and unlocked new powers in the individual, so we, too, untrammeled may yet harness the forces of hate for our own salvation. Meanwhile the drums beat discordant sounds because the new generation has not yet found the basic dynamics of their lives. But man must quickly find a means of controlling hatred for his welfare rather than for his damnation.

Love and hate are rarely far apart, although of opposite poles.

Both must be embraced, for only thus may one be master of his own soul. By recognizing and reconciling the bad in man's lot as well as the good, he can grasp a universal identity that allows him without deception to take a rightful place in the scheme of things, with the rhythm of the seasons, the ruthless swing of the stars, the fixed course of distant planets as well as the pragmatic music of his own destiny. Hate at last is confronted and fully acknowledged because it is so frequently inherent in the human soul. Only by thus getting rid of a false self, by admitting the real rather than the hypocritical may a person at last gain his real identity.

Aggression is an energy that can be harnessed against discordant elements for the betterment of mankind and for renewed mental health in the individual. Yes, even hate can be a drive for mastery, to involvement in great events, to vested interest in the improvement of one's fellowmen, instead of being turned against life itself where it can only eat into the personality. The individual must not permit himself to be alone, alienated, and shriveled into mental illness. He must act, assuming full responsibility for his own salvation.

Hate can be softened, diffused, when one struggles in worthwhile endeavors. It can be used as a source of energy against injustices and other evils. We must confront squarely our own hatreds and hostilities, acknowledge them rather than repress them. We must realize that the hypocrisy in which we clothe our hates succeeds in creating facades, false selves, masks that hide the ugly features etched by our frustrations. A society is civilized and a person is humanized to the extent that hatred and danger are channeled into creativity and the betterment of fellow beings as against primal outlets that are cruel and destructive.

Unfortunately, sometimes a person or even a nation has to learn that destructive expression of anger and hatred can bring such retribution and pain that a constructive course is finally deemed wiser. The reformed criminal who has profited from his imprisonment may thereafter choose better behavior. The former drug addict who has suffered enough without totally destroying himself may decide to rehabilitate other addicts, to help them find a new life. The car thief who has had a run-in with the law after an accident as he sought to escape may thereafter earn the money to buy his own automobile. It is therefore not uncommon for learning to evolve from prior suffering.

Thus it was in World War II after Germany and Japan unleashed their anger against other nations. After much pain and disaster following the greatest mass murder in history, these countries rose up from their ashes to become two of the most productive nations in the Western world.

Similarly, neurotic men and women must feel deeply the harm that their anger inflicted upon them before they can progress to a more effective means of handling their hostilities. The person who is unaware of his anger because it has been repressed cannot channel that anger into acceptable and socially desirable behavior.

The person who has rationalized his contention that he is without anger is more subject to emotional stress than he who recognizes that there is evil in all of us. In one sense, before being a good human being one must first admit that a devil dwells within himself.

In other words, it has to be declared that anger is an emotion that can be destructive, but also that it can be a tool for the improvement of oneself and one's neighbors as well as the world in general. People who achieve much in their lives—the great artists, the top professionals, the powerful entrepreneurs as well as the outstanding statesmen, are frequently intense haters of failure, of injustice and ugliness. They abhor disorder and love the opportunity to attack what in their opinion should be detested. The socialist hates the free-enterprise system; the capitalist hates the regimentation of the dictatorship.

It is as important to know what to hate as to know what to love. To feel both is to recognize the total self without deception, and then preferably to act according to that knowledge.

First, the individual should determine what factors in his environment or within himself are conducive to great frustrations. Frequently the environment itself can be changed, such as removing oneself from bad companions, a decaying neighborhood, a nagging parent or wife, a negative relationship with siblings or friends. Discovering unduly frustrating aspects of oneself is more difficult, since these are frequently buried deep in the subconscious. Reading self-help books may unearth some knowledge of value. Frank discussion with trusted peers may reveal partially the hidden defenses that no longer are workable. Sometimes consultation with a qualified and licensed psychologist may be necessary. The aim is primarily to uncover the chronic frustrations that inevitably must cause anger— sometimes severe enough to cause great discomfort.

With that knowledge comes the realization that all anger is justified. The modifying factor is that the way it is expressed determines welfare or damnation. Without frustration, there can be no anger. Without anger, there is no frustration.

Frustration and anger are twins, existing side by side. Both in extremes are deadly. Yet paradoxically, a little of the two is required for a full life. If we were suddenly deprived of all frustration, there would be no incentive to struggle, to achieve, even to change our world for a better existence. If frustration provides the urge for a better existence through the removal of some of it that may be in excess, anger is the motive power that helps to reduce some of that frustration. Poets have long expressed the fact that happiness is greatest after unhappiness. A rose is most beautiful when viewed against a backdrop of ugliness.

However, we need not worry that life will extend too little frustration. The mere act of living itself is frustrating. In a degree merely being hungry is frustrating, and being jilted in love is more painful. The only organism completely free of frustration is a dead one. The complementary anger is the engine that is never entirely lacking as we struggle for our well-being, for the things necessary to keep us alive, to battle obstacles. This endless pushing is never absent even in routine disappointments such as being denied a kiss from a loved one. Thus ordinary happenings arouse at least mild anger, which is felt not only as frustrating but also sometimes disguised as sadness.

Admitting, then, the prevalent anger as a result of frustration, we must seek to reduce that frustration by persisting in expending the energy stirred by anger. We can reach for love, for a meaningful career, and a way of improving ourselves and mankind. The process begins at birth and ends only with the grave. Anyone seeking to avoid that struggle is denying life itself.

On the other hand, there is joy and happiness in living actively, utilizing anger toward the continuing challenge of frustration in our changing world.

CHAPTER IV

The Hurt of Yesteryear

Most people who seek psychological help and counseling do not understand the nature of their anger. Some are submissive or withdrawn. These are the ones who have repressed their hostility and are discouraged and lonely, without hope. Yet they reach out for some magic formula that will restore their peace of mind. Others are openly bitter, rebellious, and even vicious. They may consciously hate their parents, or sometimes they transfer their anger to society as a whole, accusing the whole world of rottenness and deception.

The flaring up of hate during the teenage years is generally found to have its origin earlier in life. Perhaps the hurt of growing up had remained mute and unrecognized in childhood only to be re-awakened with the advent of sexual awareness.

In any case, it has sometimes been deemed necessary to recall and relive in therapy some of the traumatic experiences of the past. This is a painful process, but the patient has to trace the origin of his distorted anger. The present hatreds and rebellion have their roots in the past, and it is in the past that these roots must be exposed. Self-understanding and the reasons for his anger merge to release the person from the harmful effects of former years, the enslaving hurt that has been twisted into harmful neuroses.

The many euphemisms that cover up the conflicts of the childhood years are deceptive and misleading. Great frustrations confront the young person at the very beginning of life and often continue increasingly demanding as he grows older. By the time he has reached youth he has been buffeted about emotionally, sinned against, and perhaps framed in the neurotic picture of other people's expectations. In short, he has been taught to hate cunningly as the price of survival. Hypocrisy has been forced upon him as a weapon when he concealed his anger behind simulation of eating disorders and the whimpering of defeat.

He must, of course, in his primitiveness be very angry, rebellious, and even vaguely tempted to kill those who would shape him ac-

25

cording to their own whims. But sooner or later he must surrender and actually love those who make the rules. It is the only safe way. And so the child frequently becomes passive instead of rebellious, loving instead of hateful.

His drives, however, cannot be denied forever. Although they are held in check through fear and imposed love, the day will come when the energy imprisoned now will emerge in a variety of outlets, even as a teenager in street crimes or riots, really not knowing why because the reasons lie so far back when he was changed from a little animal to a nice boy. Thus he became civilized enough to survive in our culture.

By the time he has reached six years of age, his basic personality structure has been comparatively fixated, with the scars of many trauma in his being. Later, no matter how liberated he considers himself to be, no matter how he professes freedom and determination to "do his thing," he may still be ridden with repressed hatred. The hurt of the past remains to bedevil him from his subconscious.

The infant is indeed subject to frustration, anxieties, and depression. Self-preservation demands that he lay about him, beating his every limb, fighting for the breath of life, and in the first great frustrations he must emerge with the genesis of hate. Thus, according to Rebecca West, is initiated the habit of hostility against one's environment as a means of survival. Later the child will be taught that aggression as a positive force to ward off evil is itself a greater evil that must be expiated with a sense of guilt. The fact is that the child does not have to learn how to hate. He comes into the world fully equipped with the instinct to fight for and against his environment, thus possessing within his being the power of aggression as a tool for survival.

Little children will often wreak havoc on their playmates, as if it were natural to bite, kick, pull one another's hair, steal toys, and otherwise engage in over-aggressive play such as pulling out legs and arms of dolls. Unfortunately, perhaps the more their independence and resourcefulness develop, the more their antisocial demeanor tends to increase. Indeed, the spirit of the little child yields to aggressive impulses in the same manner that some adults seek by whatever means to destroy their fellow humans in war and in the cut-throat competition of some business practices and policies.

This uninhibited desire to hurt and destroy undergoes tremendous changes if the child is to be "adjusted" and made to function in organized society. Generally the infant's desire to inflict pain and to annihilate must be restricted, gradually suppressed, and finally repressed almost entirely from his consciousness. However, excessive inhibition of aggressive tendencies by overzealous but well-meaning parents may engender a pacifism and passivity that later can deny their offspring the will to self-defense and the courage to protect their own rights.

On the other hand, there is always the danger that the destructive desires will be rekindled, break out from the subconscious, and release the primitive urges. Society tries to prevent this with various defensive devices such as pity, hesitation, and consideration for the suffering of others.

One of the child's first decisions is to cry or to swallow. This choice is hard to reconcile. Both cannot be done at the same time. Is it equally difficult for him to love the person who presents her breasts and to hate the same person who takes them away? In any case, the mother inevitably must arouse both positive and negative feelings in her offspring. How can anger be thwarted without entirely obliterating the urge to aggression for positive ends, for adventure, for the creativity and the impulse to mold the world nearer to one's desire?

The newborn takes over the physiological responsibility of purifying his own bloodstream through his lungs and kidneys. Thus he begins to absorb oxygen, to exhale carbon dioxide. He drinks a watery solution of fat, sugar, and protein, and he excretes the by-products. This, then, is an organism with an energy system. The way in which this energy is disposed or stifled gives rise to desires, fears, hopes, despair—and hate.

The sound of the mother's voice, her nearness, her odor, the sweetness of her milk form the conceptual sense of love and well-being. In their deprivation lies a great frustration and the intensification of anger. The greatest difficulty in bringing up children in our culture is to persuade them to forgo present pleasures for distant goals. Restrictions that are accompanied by parental hostility create bitterness and confusion in the child. According to Karl Menninger, these discouragements cause some children to give up the idea of growing up, and they become irresponsible weaklings. Parents frequently treat their children as they were treated, thus realizing long-deferred hatreds and revenge for past indignities. The inhibited hatreds in parents are sometimes visited on the children. According to Erik H. Erickson, "Some day maybe there will exist a well-informed, well-considered, and yet fervently public conviction that the most deadly of all possible sins is the mutilation of a child's spirit . . ."

Among the crimes committed against children are inconsistency, threats, objections to disturbing activities, refusal of reasonable requests, ignoring of the child when he seeks to be pleasing, quarreling with him over unimportant matters, imposing one's own anxieties and worries upon him, discussing him in front of others, neglecting him, bribing him, lying to him, shielding him from the consequences of his own acts, comparing him unfavorably with others, inculcating attitudes of dishonesty and hypocritical philosophy of life, overprotection to compensate for the hatred of the child—and finally physical abuse and many other acts that rightfully arouse the child's hostility. Jeanne Lampl-de Groot wrote in the *Psychoanalytic Review:* "We know that the little child holds parents responsible for his distress and losses, and he responds to all sorts of pain with hatred and death wishes toward his parents."

No previous experiences are ever lost or completely obliterated. The repressed anger, the hurt and indignation remain to haunt the individual's behavior, thoughts, and emotions in the years to come. Perhaps a teenager later embraces extreme nonconformity, thus advertising the wounds of former years that are still festering. Thousands of young people each year run away from home. Even as an older adult, one carries on his back an invisible and angry child who demands retribution and a penalty for past suffering.

It would be wondrous if all parents loved their children as the sentimentalists and songwriters would have us believe. Of course, many of these offspring are unwanted in the first place. Child neglect in our society is phenomenal, contrary to the vaunted claim that nothing is too good for our children.

Some of the American Indian tribes were shocked and bewildered as they observed whites beating their children. It was difficult for these so-called savages to understand why white babies were allowed to cry until they were blue in the face. Such cruelty, the Indians surmised, was all part of a missionary zeal to impress white children with the idea that the world was indeed bad, that this fact must be impressed on children, that one must look only to an afterlife for happiness.

About two-thirds of the children needing psychiatric care in the

United States are not receiving it, according to a National Institute of Mental Health report. It was found that about 10 percent of all children need psychological help for emotional problems.

Hundreds of thousands of these children live or will live in institutions, more than 6 million of them under age fourteen now live apart from at least one parent, and many others are residing with neither parent.

Statistics indicate that broken homes appear to be increasing, and there is much evidence that mental illness in children tends to be higher in poverty areas. In addition, the medical profession reports that approximately 20 to 40 percent of all children suffer from one or more handicaps or chronic ailments. Half of the children under fifteen years of age in the United States have never visited a dentist. Eleven million children between the ages of five and seventeen have eye disorders that need treatment. Two million children have untreated hearing defects. Another two million children have orthopedic problems that remain without medical attention, and three million have speech disorders that are similarly neglected.

Each year almost a million children pass through this country's court system, detention facilities, and training schools. Many of them are guilty of only mild delinquency, but too many will be graduated from these institutions as hardened criminals.

The not uncommon hatred of some parents for their children is nowhere more evident than in the prevalence of child abuse. These parents are among the many throughout the country who each year brutally maltreat thousands of children. A considerable number of the abused die, or are paralyzed, physically deformed or mentally retarded for their remaining days. Examples of brutality are in our daily newspapers and in the courts. A mother tearfully described how her husband had finally destroyed their seven-year-old son. "On the day the boy died," she recounted, "he had so many bruises all over his hands, face, and legs." She continued her story in court, testifying that before the child died, he had said, "Daddy, I don't want to live anymore." The father had replied, "Why don't you die?" The boy answered, "All right—I will."

Similar records are on file by the thousands, a terrifying record of parents' inhumanity to their children. Beatings and other abuses are said to cause more deaths among children than such diseases as leukemia, muscular dystrophy, cystic fibrosis, and auto accidents.

In the nation's capital, a blue-eyed little girl, four years old, was admitted to the hospital. Examination revealed a fractured skull, lacerations on back, face, arms, and legs. "Mama kept hitting me with a big black stick," the child said.

Such cases are not unusual. Youngsters hardly out of the cradle and up to age sixteen are regularly admitted to hospitals with face, legs, and arms—and other parts of the body—swollen from parent-inflicted burns or beatings. "Life in the raw," Erik H. Erickson said, "drives people into being each other's persecutors, beginning with the indoctrination of children."

Those who in rationalization look upon childhood and the teen-age years as always happy times have perhaps largely repressed their own early conflicts, the hurt, and the smothered anger. The mind tends to forget the harrying experiences, savoring only the good times, as witnessed in those who love to talk about their childhood with assumed fond memories, forgetting the boredom, the indignities sometimes visited upon them, and the mute cries in the privacy of their inner selves.

Sins against younger people are rooted in prior frustrations of adults. The average middle-class citizen wants to forget that many young people actually are hungry in this affluent land. Indeed, the desperation of hunger cannot be entirely denied. It peers from the haunted eyes of the malnourished in the ghettos and rural areas, and perhaps spills over ultimately in senseless lawlessness in dimly lighted streets.

Eddie presented a dismal picture as he waited in my reception room. Although only twenty-one years old, he weighed 216 pounds and his bloated face expressed submission, broken only by a glimmer of suspicion and hostility. To him, the world indeed was a fearful place. Finally, his wife of eight months had persuaded him to see a psychiatrist, who gave him pills that succeeded only in making him physically ill.

In the early sessions of his therapy, he reluctantly began to open up with a mixture of pleading and utterances of despair. In his job in a large business office, he felt that his colleagues laughed behind his back at his awkward bulk, his cringing behavior as he went through his daily routine. His resentment of fellow workers was intense, yet he felt like an outcast allowed only to exist on the precarious rim of reality.

At home, although his wife loved him, he was unable to function sexually except marginally with oral sex and masturbation. Accordingly, he felt completely devoid of masculinity, although there were no signs of homosexuality either potential or overt.

Here was a young man filled with anger expressed through petulance, but within very strict limits because of his fear of greater rejection. On the surface, the frustrations were clear enough. He was too fat. Even women seemed to avoid him as if he carried the plague. He functioned in passive acceptance and shame for his sorry lot. In his household, he rarely laughed, more often acting like a snarling and wounded beast, unconsciously blaming his wife for the sexual problem that troubled their marriage.

Of deeper significance were the subconscious conflicts aroused long ago with the accompanying anger rarely completely recognized or expressed suitably. Early in his childhood, he had learned that his mother had conceived against her will. Also, he had developed a feeling of inferiority that was repeatedly implanted by unwise if not viciously inclined parents.

His mother, as though reaching out to make up for her frequent neglect of the boy's welfare, urged him to eat until he would feel that his stomach was about to burst. To feed her offspring doubtless carried a symbolic meaning for herself, a defense against her personal neurosis. Fat early became associated with his mother and therefore with femininity. To gain weight became fixed in his consciousness as submission in response to his mother's wish. It became a defense against threats of total rejection. To be fat was a way of identifying with the feminine world and therefore a precarious means of avoiding his mother's rejection.

Opposed to this desire to remain infantile in an attempt to gain his mother's protection, to hold on to her apron strings, was the natural wish of a boy for masculinity, to be like his father—whom in fact he hated, because the man was a competitor for the mother's attention. He visualized his parents in bed having sexual intercourse. His masturbation, which became more frequent and compulsive as he grew older, was accompanied by aggressive and punitive thoughts. Although psychologists generally consider masturbation harmless, in this case it proved to be a means of competing with the father. The act was accompanied by or carried an overtone of sadism, which in turn created in him a more intense feeling of guilt. Symbolically he not only was competing with the father in his sexual fantasies, but also imagined that he was at the same time killing him.

And so as a young adult he could not have complete sexual relations with a woman because deep within him the penetration of any woman was a replay of his early desire to have sex with his own mother. All men with whom Eddie came in contact, on the other hand, were potential attackers who would punish him for his secret thoughts—while at the same time despising him for lack of masculinity. So he went about his work with head bowed, a man almost completely defeated. Increasingly this sense of inferiority held him as though in a straitjacket of frustration. The anger that had its origin in years when he had been too weak to find his own way was ever present. His parents fed him not only an excess of food, but also a repeated diet of criticism and emotional neglect when he needed most to be loved wisely.

The lengthy therapy had its ups and downs during which he brought to the surface many of the early frustrations, the anger, the guilt, and finally the depression that had hung over his life like a pall. Recognizing his hostility and its real meaning, he projected it again and again on the therapist, blaming him for the turbulent emotions. At last he realized that his obesity was symbolic of his desire to remain an infant. He grasped the fact that his anger had been originally directed at his father, envying his masculinity, and hating him because he felt also that the father had robbed him of his manhood.

Without any specific direction that he do so, he lost weight, went down to 175 pounds. Now that he emotionally acknowledged his earlier incestuous desires, he began for the first time to enjoy normal sexual relations.

Now he held his head high, replaced his old clothes with youthful flair, talked to women who were amazed at his transformation. He viewed himself as masculine and handsome—both of which he was.

This brief case history illustrates vividly how early frustration followed by bottled-up anger can lead to guilt and finally to depression. Early hurt and emotional deprivation often remain to haunt adulthood, clinging to the personality, to create a psychological hell. Fortunately, that sequence can be curtailed with new understanding of past deprivation and a grasping of the nature of anger when it fails to find a suitable outlet.

CHAPTER V

Shades of Rebellion

The mass media keep up a constant bombardment of the message that today's young people are rebellious, drug-ridden, promiscuous, and aberrant. Many parents sit in anxious silence, guilt-tinged at this image of their pot-smoking and independent offspring. Professor K. Rose Toole, whose remarks were reprinted in the *Congressional Record,* expressed the sentiment of many middle-aged people by saying, "I am sick of the young generation, hippies, yippies, militant and nonsense . . . "I am sick of total irrationality of the campus rebel whose bearded visage, dirty hair, body odor, and tactics are not only childish, but brutal, naive, dangerous, and the essence of arrogant tyranny—the tyranny of the spoiled brat."

It is true that youth movements have come and gone, but because of the vast exposure by modern means of communication only recently has rebelliousness of young people been taken so seriously and become so disconcerting. It would even seem to be unfashionable not to be an avant garde and accept with complacency some adolescent idiocy. This, of course, reflects on the parents' lack of security and certainly on their scale of values, and gives rise to suspicion that today's youth may have valid reasons for hostility against established norms. Certainly, it is asserted, the problem began with the parents themselves. Their own growing permissiveness was a reflection of the mid-1950's trend against demands of rearing children with consistency.

The need to guide children into constructive ways to express aggression was too little understood or heeded. It was largely overlooked that although anger must find an outlet, such hostility should be vented with responsibility. The pseudo-freedom embraced was largely without responsibility—yielding a temporary sense of satisfaction until it was finally realized that without limits there is no freedom. $89-17008$

It is indeed the thesis of this book that anger should be expressed;

Lourdes High School Library
4034 West 56th Street
Chicago, Illinois 60629

but it is also reiterated that hostility should have a social aim conducive to the welfare of the person and of his fellowman.

Many of our traditional values were an outgrowth of a patriarchal and agrarian culture that stressed discipline, hard work, and the fulfillment of pledges. In that society, youth learned the performance of duty, which in turn brought its own rewards. The young person in that milieu was a supportive member of the family and the group. These values today, we are told, are not as relevant as they were for past generations.

After an exhaustive look at the Western world, George Desmotte, Social Science Director of the French National School of Public Health, found that "gone is the omnipotent husband, the father invested with unshared authority." Events are on the march to shatter ancestral traditions.

It has been pointed out that the decline in the norms of past generations really began with the industrial revolution almost two centuries ago. The importance of the family was lessened as other organizations assumed the functions previously entirely in its domain. Also, rapid technological advancement increased family mobility, not only depriving children of the security of a stable and familiar environment, but at the same time robbing them of continuing relationships with grandparents and older relatives. Accordingly, people seized the products of the industrial revolution with little regard or concern for the consideration of personal, ecological, and social changes.

Many theologians are beginning to talk about a new morality. The injunction "Thou shall not" is not always taken seriously today. Parents are now confronted with youth rebellion without their own support of traditional values—which seemingly they tacitly question in the privacy of their self-doubt. Young people as a result have been left with an erosion of traditional guides, largely rootless, with a seminomadic family structure further weakened by the shifting role of male and female. Many parents, devoid of real moral and psychological strength, have lost their function as the lighthouse to illuminate the course of the new generation.

Some young people can therefore say that our family-based society is shaky, that it lacks distinct goals, that it offers no guidelines or limits. Youth in that situation is unable to communicate with older adults and feel left out. Intrinsically linked to this dilemma is the fact that they are often deprived of meaningful work to help establish their identity through achievement.

Of course, the older person must admit that he tends to have heavy investments in present institutions, even though he may be unaware that he has become their slaves. Still there are conflicts and doubts. Parents may have done too little, too much, or the wrong things. And yet there lurks in the minds of the older generation some envy of the vague idealism and adventurousness of the young. The parents are therefore swayed between approval and disapproval of their children's ways and attitudes.

There exists fearfully a potential anarchist in each young person who says, "I can't talk to my parents," meaning that they do not listen to him or that parents have nothing to say to the younger generation. When a teenager concludes that parents and teachers are unconscious executive organs of social power, according to Wilhelm Reich, ". . . he will begin to comprehend his misery, will deny its divine origin and begin to rebel against his parents and the powers whom they represent."

Youth finds loud voices of doom from such as Herbert Marcuse and Charles Reich and their disciples of the New Left who claim that society, while outwardly more successful than any in history, is still only a structure of naked power and covert manipulation. One finds on every major campus today a faculty group eager to complement their vocation of teaching with an activism that puzzles many people.

According to these activists, our society is unjust to its poor and the minorities; it is functioning mainly for the benefit of a privileged class, lacks true democracy and freedom. It is ugly and artificial, destructive of environment and self-identity—in fact, untruthful and hypocritical. Older people are neglected, our streets are made hideous with commercialism, and the monotony of our existence is pervaded with loneliness, while nature is devastated by bulldozers and pollution. Schools impose their stupid mindlessness, and our system of justice serves mainly the capitalistic elite. Our values are based entirely on coarse materialism. Marriages are wells of loneliness, with the individual surrounded on all sides by empty lives in empty homes.

Young people see some degree of fallacy in these contentions, but also some glimmer of truth. Many are convinced that there are many wrongs in our society. According to one study, 99 percent of 1,542 college seniors surveyed at 10 institutions thought that confrontation of some kind was necessary, with 28 percent of those willing to turn such confrontation into physical disruptions.

What are the thoughts of teenagers as they listen to their elders heaping scorn upon the society that has nurtured them? Will they be able to discern the sincere from the publicity seeker, the weak from the strong?

To gain immortality, Hierostratus burned the temple of Diana in ancient Ephesus. Today we also have our thrill and immortality seekers, and our institutions are far more widespread and vulnerable. Vandals in our times have their meaningless flings. And yet perhaps it is not the flag of anarchy that is symbolized by the stirring among young people, but the harbinger of a new day when aggression becomes a tool for social justice rather than an auxiliary by which people are kept comparatively meek and submissive.

The graffiti of youth rebellion is scrawled on bridges and public buildings as well as on toilet walls, symbolically thumbing noses at conformity. And yet young people, contrary to their claim of non-conformity, are strongly imitative. Their feelings, actions, and style tend to be uniform. To follow these trends is to be hep, in time, turned on, with it; to ignore them is to be a square, an outsider.

The way they dress, walk, and talk, their attitudes toward sex, their heroes and enemies are all one parcel of the total configuration of their culture—which is actually the utmost in dependency and conformity according to their own norms. Their language is said to be impoverished for all their contention of depth and pseudo-philosophy; it is repetitive, emphasizing their alienation, their empty political posturing.

If these accusations are true, then perhaps instead of trading one conformity for another, young people might advantageously find more positive ways of expressing their anger.

On the other hand, it is obvious that misfits and losers are hiding in unconventional clothes and beards. They are able to disguise themselves, permitting the youth movement to take the blame. In past years, bums, drifters, and emotional defectives were highly visible with their tattered clothing, glassy eyes, and unwashed odors. Today their raunchy appearance can be justified by the simple subterfuge of adorning themselves with a few beads or belts, thus passing on the onus of their noxiousness to the movement of which they pretend to be a part.

The ranks of the true progressives are infiltrated with plastic imitators who haven't the least conception of the principles that animate the movement. These masqueraders feel that they can get away with outrageous conduct, knowing that the public cannot discriminate between the earnest activist and those who use the movement to provide easy and safe targets for discharging nasty aggression, anxiety, and hate.

Malcolm Muggeridge commented on the behavior of such individuals. "How sad," he said, "how macabre that so many young people have sought escapism through the method that is the resort of old, slobbering debauchees anywhere in the world at any time— dope and bed."

And yet the more we publicize delinquency, the more we associate it with evil, the more it becomes dramatic and heroic for some emotionally disturbed persons. The glamor of wickedness and danger is a distorted way of striving for identity and a sad sort of achievement. The mass media, together with some confused or complacent parents and insecure educators, have done what the young generation could never have accomplished on its own, namely, the acceptance of degeneracy as something intrinsically acceptable. Some cynical young people have had help from their detractors in challenging all values.

While lack of new frontiers has driven many to alcohol, drugs, and glue-sniffing, their parents have no less been without meaningful goals. Success for its own sake, the job as the dominant aspect of life, the competitive race, and the pursuit of money as the most important objective in life, all combine to make cynics of many people.

Young people do not seem to smile as readily today. Perhaps they are paying too high a price for their rebellion. Maybe in spite of their bravado there are too numerous frustrations beneath the veneer of their pretensions. Of the estimated 100,000 heroin addicts in New York City, there were 900 heroin deaths in a recent year, a quarter of them teenagers. A sprawled and lifeless figure of a girl with limbs awry in the hallway of a ghetto dwelling is not a pretty picture nor one to allay the adult guilt over our failure to meet vital needs for a young person's sense of identity, for a feeling of worth and dignity.

The current fad for long hair and beards among young people may denote a return to an earlier and more primitive level of existence, or perhaps to a more natural way of life. According to the psychiatrist Karl A. Menninger, the practice of shaving and cutting one's hair is a sort of self-mutilation as a concession to the aesthetic value of a civilized community.

Hair and sexual aggression are closely associated, as exemplified in the story of Samson and Delilah. That hair in part represents virility is apparent in the popular conception of the hairy-chested man in such plays as Eugene O'Neill's *The Hairy Ape* and the more recent *Hair*.

One factor that seems to increase misunderstanding in the older generation is the fear of youth's sexuality and fighting spirit. And yet almost our entire cultural production as expressed in art, literature, poetry, dance, drama, and other media is deeply characterized by interest in sex.

The length of a person's hair, according to researchers, frequently has been associated with other meanings in the past. Egyptian travelers, for example, allowed their hair to grow long until the end of a long journey. Upon reaching manhood, the Greek youth made an offering of his hair to a local river; and Achilles wore his hair long because his father had vowed it to the river Sperchius if his son returned safely from the war. Among the Nazarites, hair-cutting was prohibited during a religious festival.

The American Indian, too, considered hair to be symbolic. Like the Greeks, they believed hair to be the seat of life. The scalp represented the essence of the individual. It was an insult for another merely to touch it lightly. And scalping, of course, was the ultimate indignity. Among the Franks, caste was shown by the manner in which hair was worn—even as many of our young people today indicate their status and uniqueness by the length of their hair. In the distant past, short hair marked the slave in contrast to the long locks of the free man, just as in our culture the neat haircut generally denotes the establishment, whereas the abundance of hair is deemed removed from it.

In some European countries, shaving the head was a severe punishment for women who fraternized with the enemy during World War II. The same penalty was once meted out for adultery in India and among the Teutons, and for other offenses among the Babylonians. One may note that the heads of prisoners are often shorn, perhaps symbolizing the loss of liberty and individuality.

The popularity of the hairdressing business, with its catering to the eroticism of hair, is evidence of its implication in sexual attraction. With older men, the attempt to rationalize baldness with virility bears witness to the importance of hair in the relationship between men and women.

Our preoccupation with hair has its pathological side in hair fetishism, when a person derives sexual gratification by merely admiring and caressing hair to the exclusion of any more direct physical contact. Such a person wants the hair and nothing else. Police in every city are familiar with the hair stealer or "clipper" who will surreptitiously cut a lock of a woman's hair without seeking any further contact with his victim.

While having one's hair caressed, dressed, and improved in appearance are not without pleasure, cutting off hair has often been looked upon as renunciation of power. It used to be, for example, that the most precious personal adornment possessed by Chinese was the queue, and having it cut off was tantamount to total disgrace and disaster.

Hair in our society has many meanings. It can indeed be rebellion in the shock of flowing hair and beard. In any case, it is a harmless sort of aggression. It may also be the assertion of one's identity and individuality without denying others the same right to be themselves.

Although elders may decry youth's conformity in wearing blue jeans, medals, belts, and other accoutrements, they in turn are gradually eliminating the uniform of tie, white shirt, and blue or gray suit in the business office—as if timidly seeking to imitate the younger set. Perhaps the two generations will ultimately grow closer to each other.

Meanwhile, it must be assumed that if younger people are denied some degree of rebellion, one of the main dynamics of self-realization is blocked, with resultant frustration. However, a young person must have some limitations on his conduct. Such rules become something to rebel against. As we attain adulthood, we may wish that our parents had been more firm and more consistent in discipline. The overlenient parent failed essentially because the environment provided no opportunity for rebellion.

Anger against established norms can lay the foundation for personal growth and experimentation. This axiom is difficult for some people to accept. Their concept of a good adolescent is one who follows precisely in his parents' footsteps. He dutifully enters his father's business, studies to be a teacher because his elders deemed it an honored profession, or makes the dreams of his parents come true. Many who follow this well-worn path are repaid with much frustration because they have not been allowed to stand on their own feet, thus disallowing any forms of rebellion.

Of course, it must not be assumed that young people who go into their father's business or profession are always doomed to severe frustration and its aftermath. Nevertheless, it must be granted that sufficient independence should be provided to permit self-development. A sense of worthiness and strength can be achieved only by some degree of rebellion. This is necessary to offset the long years of dependency of the Western child before he reaches manhood.

Anger against the establishment, however, tends to lessen as the years make increasing practical demands. It is understandable that someone under eighteen can with impunity exercise his need to challenge the rights of others. It is also clear that he will be more careful in later years, knowing that he must arrive safely at his job in order to support wife and family. The rebels of the 1960's are generally established as solid citizens today.

A mild spirit of rebellion impels the young person to make his own decisions, choosing his own course whether it be following the wishes of his parents or doing the opposite. Parents and other significant figures may help in arriving at these decisions by sharing their experiences. But it is important that a young person determine the role he will play in life. That course of action must be chosen independently, without pressure. The wise parent realizes that even idiosyncrasies in young people may be only a necessary step or stage in their development. A so-called fling of seeming irresponsibility is only temporary in the average adolescent. On the other hand, if this period of rebellion does not take place, then in later life immaturity may persist because rebellion has been denied in earlier years.

Does this mean that young people should be permitted free rein on their drive for independence? They might be the last to admit that complete permissiveness is desirable. In fact, lack of intelligent and patient guidance on the part of the parents often leads young people to seek more discipline and regimentation on their own. They frequently find these in cults that demand such intense discipline that it amazes older people.

Why does a young person willingly give up his freedom, becoming a slave to some questionable religious and dictatorial guru? Such a leader may be viewed as God's representative on earth—if not actually God himself. Celibacy and complete submission are imposed upon cult-loving young people. Their minds respond to a strange music that draws them to a level never before experienced. Their ears remain open only to the arbitrary teaching of a master.

Is it not puzzling that so many thousands should seek a masterful liberator, a system, who and which impose complete obedience at a time when only yesterday they proclaimed the evil of a society that stifled freedom? Is it possible that they reacted with disappointment when their demands were met by their elders?

Are they now saying that they have a right to choose even their own type of slavery? Or is it rather that all along they thirsted for some moral values that were found wanting in the older generation? Our churches, which originally served as the core of moral guidance, are now being emptied of young people as traditional religious leaders drop strict dogma and replace it with sociological aims. "Look," some ministers, priests, and rabbis say, "we are becoming modern. We want to appeal to young people by getting rid of the old." The Bible is modernized, the clergy speaks street talk, going out in Times Square to preach social justice—while God often remains behind.

Young people may want more of the old, the sincerity and the lack of hypocrisy, than we dream of. If elders do not believe in their own values, how can they challenge rebellion on the part of the young? Dictators and cult leaders know well enough the hunger that exists in young people for a clear voice making clear demands for sacrifice and devotion. Perhaps the young did not really want what they proclaimed they wanted. Paradoxically they may be saying, "Give us something worthwhile to rebel against. Thus establishing our identity, we could then return to the old faiths after we have had our fling. However, by misinterpreting our rebelliousness, you destroy not only the perpetuation of whatever faith you may still retain, but also leave us no refuge to which we might have returned."

It is little wonder that young people yield their minds to cult leaders who, if they are swindlers in moral values, still offer something that elders are no longer capable of providing. If God is dead, older people have killed him.

Perhaps out of changes that baffle them, the new generation may yet show the way out of the confusion of elders by creating their own scale of values and new rules that they can break but that will remain as a refuge when the fire of their rebellion has died down. Their home will not have disappeared as they wandered for a while like the prodigal son. They will in the process have found their identity. Their idols will then be more real than those of their fathers because they will not be an alloy of expediency, but endowed with consistency and worthy of respect.

CHAPTER VI

Aggressive Sexuality

It would seem, according to many sexologists, that the more sex one has the better it is for physical and mental health. That contention or implication is obviously questionable. It is not the frequency of sex that is important, but rather the quality. Promiscuity can be the sign of emotional disorders rather than the expression of masculinity or femininity. However, to deny that there is a new sexual freedom among young people would be equally unrealistic.

This so-called liberation through sex was nowhere better exemplified than by the United Presbyterian Church in the U.S.A., after intense debate in 8,667 congregations. The resultant committee report found no theological stricture against masturbation, homosexuality, contraception, abortion, or sexual activities in the single adult.

It may be significant that practically at the same time Dr. Geoffrey Simmons reported a startling epidemic among the young, with 250 to 300 cases of gonorrhea weekly in his Los Angeles clinic. It is estimated that, for example, there are 2 million cases of this venereal disease each year in California. Perhaps this epidemic is a symptom of the spreading belief that the old standards of morality are no longer valid. Sexual promiscuity as a form of rebellion among the young may be an expression of anger and hate aroused by frustration that has not been allowed normal and acceptable channels.

Everybody in his lifetime faces concerns of sexual tensions. Sex is a pervasive and powerful force, but it is still a subject that is poorly known and understood. Certainly it is inextricably interrelated with other ecstasies, work, power, encounter with others, and mysticism.

Much has been written to trace the emergence of guilt feelings in the psychosexual development of the child. However, entirely apart from and doubtless in addition to the known psychological and physical factors that tend to produce sexual guilt, there may be an even more basic reason for the guilt easily associated with sexual intercourse. This mechanism may still subconsciously affect youth in spite of his claimed emancipation.

Sexual orgasm is nonvolitional. The behavior that accompanies it is disoriented and allied to physical and mental shock. The experience of the climax in sex leaves the person completely helpless to ward off hostile forces that could have threatened him in the dim past.

In prehistoric times this disorienting experience by a person in the height of sexual excitement may have temporarily deprived him of the capability to defend himself from sudden attack. In other words, in the throes of sexual ecstasy his advantage even over lower animals was wiped out.

Like the priest in ancient Italy who held office at the price of constant fear of being murdered, so the primitive person engaged in sex at the risk of physical helplessness against enemies. He performed the act expecting to be set upon by assailants. Thus this most intimate pleasure of man was disturbed by the possibility of being helpless against attack.

The solution came naturally to primitive man. He had to seek a cave, a hidden place to use during copulation in order to protect his life. But the defensive act of hiding generally implied two things: darkness and secrecy. These two factors are inextricably linked to taboos, fears, superstition, and anger. Man had to hide away from the light of day in order to avoid the eyes of his fellow creatures. He carried the secret of this hiding place perhaps for some time, since such a refuge could be utilized again and again. In fact, considerable evidence might be uncovered to prove that some of these hideouts for the purpose of copulation later became sites for the worship of the gods because of their safety and the emotional connotation attached to them.

From that time, the gradual transition of sex to sinful—unless sanctified by the ruling group and the priest—is easy to understand, since in the past it was so closely linked to murder, to darkness, and to secrecy.

It may seem strange, and youth may find it difficult to free himself of the unconscious impulse and prohibitions that may still be dominant in the inner recesses of his ancestral psyche. Others have pointed out experiences long past in the human race that continue in a subtle way to influence our emotional reactions. It may be that with all his bravado and claims of new freedom, a young person does not escape easily from the residue of primitive influences. Most young people would decry the contention that they are afflicted with some degree of guilt and sexual anger that were implanted by an establishment dominated by savage priests in ancient times. "We have broken down the hypocrisy of the double standard," they would say. Certainly the older generation cannot forget that they were often as promiscuous as some of their progeny—except that their forbidden activities were more hidden, less exposed in the name of emancipation.

Those of middle age may be at a disadvantage in debating with their offspring, because some of these older people are becoming more honest in recognizing their own failings. Still there remains the fact that both groups—the young and the old—are in many instances stripping away some of the obstacles that are inherently frustrating. And since frustration is the devil giving birth to hate, one must conclude that some newfound freedom—including the much publicized sexual revolution—would be a step forward in human progress. The older generation may recoil from such a conclusion because it threatens so fundamentally their sacred institutions. In regard to freer sexual behavior, however, perhaps reluctantly we must weigh Alfred C. Kinsey's statement: "In no other field of science have scientists been satisfied to accept the biological notions of ancient jurists and theologians or the analyses made by mystics of two or three thousand years ago."

We are reminded, however, that the present value system—even if it be sometimes crass and no longer completely workable—must be given a substitute scale if we are not to be left with anarchy. In other words, our aggression must be directed to purposeful goals. Our sexuality must not be merely a bestial thing. The emotion attached to the act must be sincere, tinged with love and consideration for one's partner. Man's sex drive and the aggression often connected with it must be aimed toward both the good of the individual and that of a sane society. Only by thus canalizing our basic drives can we avoid the polarizing of individual selfishness against human welfare as a whole. Raising one's fist against our culture—mere destructive hate—without positive ends and plans for a better future can only arouse counterhate, with chaos ultimately resulting.

Strike out against injustice, bigotry, and ignorance, we must. But as we march forward demanding the downfall of some doubtful values, the black flag of rebellion for the sake of destruction itself must fail us in the end.

The activist must unfurl a new banner of purposeful good for all the people, young and old, for a new day when one can stand strong, no longer held in numbing passivity, but a fighter for a new holy grail clearly defined as a unifying objective acceptable by most reasonable people of good will.

But let us be more practical and face the fact that many young people have sexual problems that cannot be resolved by platitudes and preaching. For lack of space, we shall omit discussion of venereal diseases and unwanted pregnancy and shall dwell directly on how teenagers and other young adults can evaluate and determine the source of their sexual desires. Since this is obviously our most powerful drive, it must follow that frustrations can occur.

If this powerful instinct is overlooked or completely ignored, anger, guilt, and depression are almost inevitable and serious emotional problems may arise. This does not mean that a person has to be active sexually, nor does it imply that he or she must abstain. These are moral questions over which the professional psychologist has no jurisdiction.

Before being more specific, let's examine a case history of a young woman in sexual difficulty.

Iola walked haughtily into my office with a disdainful expression. "I don't know why I'm here," she said, flicking her cigarette toward an ashtray and missing. "I know damned well you can't help me," she added, casting a critical glance toward the diplomas on the wall.

"Why did you make an appointment?" I countered, slightly annoyed by her condescension.

"All right," she yielded tentatively. "What do you want me to do?"

"That's up to you," I tossed back.

"It's sex," she said. "But I suppose many women have that problem."

"What problem?" I asked, sensing her reluctant need to talk.

The story unfolded in succeeding sessions as she gradually dropped her facade of sophistication. Her eyes clouded as she fiddled with her bracelet. As the wife of a successful publisher, she held an important position in the firm. She seemed to possess almost everything that a woman could want, beauty, a wealth of worldly goods, a famous husband. Indeed, she had much—except happiness.

Her early years had been a sad contrast with her present status.

She had been born the daughter of a poor farmer who did more drinking than farming, the eldest of seven children. At eleven she had been repeatedly raped by an uncle, who threatened to cripple her if she told anyone of the experiences. Thus she began traumatically with sex, followed by even more shocking relationships with her own father.

She and one of her sisters slept in an attic room. At night when on a drunken spree, the father would creep up the stairs and threaten both of them if either dared to yell. The mother, who lived in fear of her husband, spent much of her time in a sort of stupor, praying as she knelt before a kitchen chair, imploring forgiveness in the hereafter. However, when the girls told her of the night ravages, they were chastised for telling lies. Finally, Iola one night placed a bread knife under her pillow. When her father staggered toward the bed in the dim light of the oil lamp, she brought out the knife and pointed it at his throat. "You son-of-bitch," she yelled. "I'll kill you if you ever come here again." He suddenly became sober, and that was the last of his midnight excursions.

Coupled with this sordid background was a Cinderella story that proved even more fantastic. Iola at sixteen began to win minor beauty contests at country carnivals. Of extraordinary beauty and perfection of figure, she finally won a regional contest, after which she was approached by a New York businessman who made many promises, including freedom from home, independence, and perhaps even fame. After a series of motel rooms, she had left him with a single dress on her back and a bathing suit in her battered suitcase.

Although by this time she harbored a deep hatred for all men, she did not mind the sexual demands made by her lover. She herself felt no sensation at all in the sexual act, merely simulating orgasm to please her companion. Thereafter, one lover followed another. She sought out men who could advance her career from salesgirl to modeling in a department store. Finally, having developed a worldliness far removed from the scared existence of earlier years, she met her present husband.

"Did you continue to fake orgasm?" I asked as she hesitated in her recital.

"Of course; I had learned a long time ago that this was the way to please men," she emphasized. "But," she continued, "I had finally met a man whom I couldn't hate. I wanted to please him, too."

"Your marriage—how is it going?"

"Very well," she replied. "But I am not happy. I want to be really a woman." She looked up, pleading. "Help me," she said.

The frustration of early years had left their marks when her environment failed to provide an outlet for the anger that festered within her. It is true that she allowed herself to hate men, but her very insecurity and the long struggle prevented her from finding suitable expressions. She had to hang on to her livelihood by catering to men who had ravaged her personality. Accordingly, her anger was turned against herself; she imagined her person as ugly and repulsive in spite of the fact that her beauty had been her essential means of support. The unexpressed anger had also taken a sexual course. She was completely deprived of sensual feelings—until she met her husband, who had managed through kindness and comforting at last to arouse love. Nevertheless, she felt guilty, unclean, unworthy, and depressed.

The sequence of the neurosis had progressed in the usual way: first the frustrations, then the anger, the guilt, and finally the chronic condition of ever-pressing depression.

"Help me," she kept repeating, reaching out almost hopelessly for salvation. And the day indeed finally came after a long period of sex therapy, behavioral technique, and gentle guidance when in the natural course of events, she entered my office. "I did it—I did it," she exclaimed. "I am now a woman. Thank God, I am a woman."

Basically all sexual dysfunctions are due to anger unexpressed or expressed unwisely—engendered by frustration, unless of course such disorders are attributable to organic factors. All psychologists in private practice have in their files numerous case histories testifying to that fact.

Young people have three choices in handling their sexual drive. They may abstain, sublimate, or find a direct expression of their sexuality.

Abstention. It may appear contradictory to say that abstention from sexual activities need not necessarily lead to emotional disturbances. It is true, for example, that many celibate religious orders such as priests and nuns seem to maintain their mental health. People in far places removed from members of the opposite sex seem to survive without malignant results. Men under fire in military campaigns rarely feel the need for sex. Starving people are similarly without sexual desire.

The substitution of another instinct to replace the sexual drive can obliterate its needs. The priest who considers self-preservation in the hereafter may thus find spiritual salvation of greater significance than desires of the flesh in the present. The man whose very existence is at stake as in battle is more concerned with his immediate survival. The person whose very being depends on the next mouthful of food or water has no energy left for the secondary importance of sexual fulfillment.

Sublimation. This device is in some respects related to abstention. However, here we are speaking specifically of substituting for sex some achievement in other spheres. The person does not wait for the next world, nor does he put off his desires until after the battle or at the end of the famine. He decides instead to seek activities apart from sex for self-fulfillment. He harnesses sex energy for a greater cause, a goal that he considers more significant.

A person may be so immersed in his work that he has little time for other emotional outlets. Sports are excellent forms of sublimation. Great scientists, artists, writers, and architects have donated their achievement to the world, feeling a sense of satisfaction that is enough in itself.

However, one does not have to be famous and talented to make use of sublimation as a substitute for sexual satisfaction. It has been noted, for example, that college students are less sexually active than those with lesser education. Perhaps this is in many cases because those in higher education are working toward specific goals that are in their opinion of more importance. It is the postponement of present pleasure for greater pleasure in the future.

A sense of achievement, the doing of something worthwhile, the absorption of one's energy in meaningful tasks: sublimation can serve anyone with a will and a desire to undertake interesting endeavors. Participation in school, church, or community activity; excelling academically; or even being a skilled mechanic or tennis player may all be suitable substitutes for sexual energy.

Overt Sex. We refer here to the direct satisfaction of the sexual drive. Most common, of course, is intercourse between men and women, particularly that which brings about mutual orgasm based on natural function. To say that, apart from release of tension, such activity cannot be achieved without love is to overlook the biological urge to copulate.

It must be reiterated, however, that the greatest pleasure is derived when two are in love or at least have respect one for the other. Promiscuity may have insecurity as its foundation. It lessens the deep feelings that accompany a sincere relationship.

The two most common sources of guilt or hangup in young as well as older people are oral sex or masturbation, the first increasingly practiced, and the latter having always been with us.

In past eras, it was not uncommon for pseudopsychiatrists to write books filled with case histories purporting to prove that masturbation, learnedly identified as "self-abuse," was a direct cause of insanity. Today one wonders about the naivety of these physicians. That "old wives' tale" still lingers on even though it has long ago been proven a myth. There is in fact no harm in masturbation. It has been said that 99 percent of men have engaged in the practice and that the other 1 percent are lying. Masturbation is a natural function not only in growing up, but also as a means of releasing tension. Of course, there may be associated harm resulting from an accompanying sense of guilt engendered by neurotic symbolism imposed by other neurotic people. It might be noted that the first aim of a sex therapist when confronted with the case of a non-orgasmic female is to develop her ability to masturbate. Once this has been established, it is possible to transfer the new sensitivity thus evoked to a more satisfying sexual expression in mutual intercourse.

It would therefore seem that the manner of expressing one's sexual appetite is a personal matter that is definitely one's own responsibility and the privilege of any normal human being. Any law that seeks to invade the bedroom of adults is nearly always an abridgment of basic civil rights and therefore increasingly regarded with suspicion.

CHAPTER VII

The Black Thread

Man's progress has been compared by Sir James G. Frazer in *The Golden Bough* to a long rope woven of three colored threads —the black thread of magic, the red thread of religion, and the white thread of science. Although the white strand of science has increasingly appeared as exemplified in technological advances, still the blackness of magic is very much a part of the warp and woof of our thinking.

Although science has given rise to a mighty array of new energies, new chemical elements, television, instruments for the exploration of outer space, and a host of gadgets to lighten physical burdens, yet there remains a magical belief, a superstition that surrounds the mysteries of science and its esoteric language. The practitioners of the sciences are frequently suspected of conniving at the obliteration of mankind with their nefarious weapons of destruction and of poisoning our environment with their inventions. Scientists live in separate compartments. There is little communication between the various scientific and technical disciplines and the average person.

That person acknowledges what the scientist does, sees evidence of his work all around him, but he does not know what the scientist knows, and he does not understand the technical terms. Accordingly, there must always be a wall between the scientist and others because the scientist cannot meet their psychological need to understand. The deeper we go into the atom, and the farther we penetrate the universe, both the microcosm and the macrocosm display mysteries that defy the rational logical explanation of most people. The mind of the average man seems to be stunned by facts that he feels are beyond his comprehension or control.

With the gradual receding of the red thread of religion as a predominant power in Western civilization, and the increasing emergence of the white thread of science less understood by the populace, there remains the black tissue of magic upon which one seeks a reestablishment of earlier security. One seems to be drawn pell-

51

mell into a new primitiveness and in many cases actually into anarchy in the midst of the greatest scientific progress in history.

Those who have studied the characteristics of magical thinking have noted that this primitive device is far from being consistent. A person, for example, while denying superstition, may nevertheless avoid an important undertaking on Friday the 13th, and hotels and hospitals also refuse to number a floor the 13th. It would seem that a person's conscious intellect rejects magic while his subconscious mind still holds on to a deeper, less logical belief.

A second characteristic of our ancestors' way of thinking—still far from being removed in our society—is the tendency to believe in the omnipotence of thought. For example, a person may know by logic that fantasies of death do not in any way invite disaster. Yet there still persists in the inner layer of his mind the belief that certain thoughts may bring evil. "Do not imitate a cripple," a child may be warned, "because you may be punished by becoming one yourself."

A third remnant of magical thinking is that of confusing thinking with doing. We shall become rich tomorrow because we mix fact with fantasy. That kind of thinking sells millions of lottery tickets.

The fourth characteristic of primitive thinking that still lurks within our minds is the importance of wishing rather than knowing; and the fifth characteristic is the tendency to equate two things because both happen to be linked with the same emotional response. This trap of similarity in magical thinking is exemplified in the conclusion that because Harvard University has graduated many outstanding scholars, it must follow that attending that institution will automatically make one a scholar. Also, because using a certain deodorant seems to make others lucky in love, it must follow—as the advertisers so ruthlessly claim—that I, too, can be a successful lover by merely changing my scent.

As we consider this type of thinking, we naturally associate it with the mentality of savages in distant lands and times. But actually it is within ourselves, in our subconscious, practically unchanged from that which existed in the Stone Age.

In primitive man, his subconscious was blurred with reality, his world was peopled by imaginary powers and beings. The life of modern man is presumed to be somewhat less influenced by his subconscious because early in his childhood he has been taught to repress much. Nevertheless, many of our conscious thoughts are still colored by the primitive subconscious. We are made aware of this psychological pathology in spite of ourselves in dreams, neurotic symptoms, fantasies, and in criminality and mental disorders. Jean Piaget emphasized all these by referring to them as "fragments of internal references which cling to the external world."

The study of human behavior as a science has come about within the short span of scarcely more than a century. Even the so-called psychology of the Greeks was little more than the exorcising of an incarnated devil. Later, John Weyer, sometimes called the father of modern psychiatry, regarded the "demoniacal world about him as an enormous clinic teeming with sick people." He made little differentiation among the insane, criminals, witches, and heretics.

The magic of the primitive mind is certainly still real enough. Only in the past 50 years has our approach to mental health sought to understand the significance of impulses that may be deeply buried within us. Indeed superstition and magic still cling to some extent in the medical profession as doctors grope hesitantly in dealing with emotional distress and mental illnesses. This primitive way of thinking, therefore, is not confined to ignorant people, to children, or to the insane. It still stalks at times in professional offices, intruding everywhere, even upon the scientist when he is removed from his formula and his laboratory.

Few of us would deny that ideas of past ages exist side by side with the latest scientific thought. The discovery of amazing devices—the spectroscope, the interferometer, and sensitive instruments to measure distant planets—are part of our daily news, but the same newspapers probably also run astrology columns. Some people entrust their wealth to stargazers and their health to quacks of various kinds.

Perhaps the idea of the "teeming clinic" is not entirely fallacious when one considers localities crowded with mentally sick people, with crime lurking in the streets, character disorders, and a complacency sometimes bordering on nihilism.

Of course, our ancestors created the devil as a symbol of the evil that they externalized on a vast screen of their own self-deception. The "devil" is still with us, but we have a slightly different conception of him. He is our own evil desires, uncontrolled hate, and antisocial urges that we have refused to acknowledge fully, have repressed from our consciousness until they break out to work havoc upon society in murders and other crimes.

Many people, therefore, exist in our highly technological society with scant knowledge of its actual workings, yet dominated by emotional responses and attitudes that have changed little in centuries. The hate of today's citizens may be just as intense as that of primordial times—perhaps more so because of the stress of a highly artificial and demanding environment.

There are those who claim naively that man's hatred has been learned, that in a civilized milieu there should be no hostility, that we can unlearn the lesson of millennia past and become meek, docile, and unaggressive. Yet the admonition that we should love our neighbors as ourselves carries irony in the fact that rarely before in history has so much hatred existed. How can a person love others when he hates himself? All love begins with self-love, an eagerness to satisfy unmet needs. By hating ourselves—as a result of severe frustrations imposed by our society—we rarely can avoid hating others.

If indeed hostility and aggression are learned, the centuries have taught well. If, however, the tendency and inevitability of hate are instinctive in the sense that man was created with the predisposition to anger as birds are predisposed to fly, then that denial of this potent emotion is doubly impractical.

Regardless of whether hate is learned or innate, the fact remains that frustration does arouse hostility. That simple fact is what concerns us. The search for a way to lessen that anger or to express it constructively must be sought. It cannot be denied or repressed except at grave risk to our mental health.

It is sometimes asserted that in the dimness of prehistoric eras man ran greater risks and had less chance of surviving. Yet by simply referring to the mounting tolls of homicides, wars, and the countless other threats to modern man's existence, that contention may easily be challenged. Coupling the confusion and the lack of understanding that beset us can easily emphasize the precarious position of urban man.

Primitive man was governed by set rules that were adhered to by most of his fellow tribesmen, and his logic was based on gods and supernatural beings who had their reasons even for bringing disasters and suffering on mankind. There was comparatively little uncertainty about the order of things. On the other hand, we tend frequently to stand devoid of the primitive orderliness possessed by our early ancestors. There is a difference between the superstition and magic of primordial people and those of modern man. Our distant ancestors believed firmly in their scheme of things, whereas we pretend not to believe in anything. Yet we may be significantly dominated by unacknowledged magic without the attendant and imaginary security which that magic brought to early man.

Our hates are still with us because we live in a predominantly frustrating society. In order to acclimate ourselves to group living by rules of technological necessities, our childhood had to be adjusted to the norms of an industrial complex, followed by adolescence that too often was denied responsibility. We then entered adulthood with lagging footsteps, often reverting in futile self-defense to earlier modes of adaptation—the neuroticism of men and women who have been baffled by seeing more than they could bear.

It is sometimes claimed there is an intrinsic inclination of a technical society to destroy itself through pollution and disregard for the individual. It is questionable whether or not the frustration and restrictions that are needed to perpetuate and to protect our society do at the same time elicit such a sickness that the society is no longer worth saving. If the meek do ultimately inherit the earth, there may be little left in it. Fortunately this is an extreme view, and certainly not one shared by those who would direct their anger toward improving our culture.

The crucial point, however, is that society may have reached a dangerous degree of frustration. The inability to express anger properly generates an undue amount of neuroticism and other character disorders. The price of progress may be inflated at a rate beyond the ability of some people to pay.

Three choices are open to us: we may accept mental illness as the cost of the privilege of existing in our society; we may give vent to our hatred through violence in order to release inner tension; or—the more difficult but the only justifiable choice—we may sublimate our hatreds and otherwise canalize them, thus harnessing hatred for human welfare rather than allowing it to run rampant for destructive purposes.

The person in this changing environment finds himself beset by increasing frustration. His job is frequently so boring that he is driven to violence. The average man's work today rarely provides a satisfactory outlet for his creative energies. Leisure time does not compensate for the monotonous factory or office employment, nor does it impel the worker to release his accompanying hostility.

It is pointed out that the sterility of industrial and technological employment is far greater than ever in human history. Consequently boredom threatens disaster unless we learn how to release tensions in a manner that is both self-satisfying and acceptable to a society in the throes of great disequilibrium.

The despair of the worker engaged day after day on an endless assembly line must ultimately exude from his pores. It is little wonder that at times he must project his anger against the machine or some imaginary exploiter embodied by society as a whole, leaving an occasional nut unscrewed, later resulting in defective products or accidents on highways. Through the magic wand of his wrench, like a destructive god, he projects his anger against an unseen and innocent enemy.

The industrial plant or factory worker is frequently worn out by the time he reaches fifty years of age. Later someone hands him a pension. If he is not an alcoholic, he may have a few more years to watch television, to live an empty life, devoid of worthwhile achievement, hardly more human than the bolts he tightened for so many years. He has become a drained vessel by the long corrosiveness of hates held too long in the bitterness of of himself.

In short, the man years ago had felt hopelessly trapped in his job, caught in an intricate web of his own and society's weaving. "What he may have lost in richness and in genuine feeling of happiness," Erich Fromm wrote, "is made up by the feeling of security he feels by fitting in with the rest of mankind." Somehow through some strange and deceiving magic, his future in the so-called golden years will be happy ones. But the gods will have retired long before he did, leaving him empty and discarded.

What then can young people do to save their sanity in a world with many signs of insanity? First they must understand the basic concept that anger is always the result of frustration, that anger if unexpressed or unwisely expended leads to depression. Nearly anyone who reaches early manhood has been the victim of that syndrome. Without full understanding and wise decisions, that sequence is inevitable, particularly among young people because of their rapid biological development and the changing world to which they are exposed.

Some frustration is assured and ever present in the mere fact of living, by the retention of myths and superstition of past ages, by living almost entirely through the devices of other generations when life was less complicated. One must therefore ever question, weigh actions in terms of one's real wants and needs. One must seek to lessen obstacles to meeting needs and thereby lessen subsequent anger—varying in degree from mild annoyance to actual hate. But we must also recognize that we can never eliminate all frustrations and accordingly can never be entirely free of anger. Once we have reduced blocks to the realization of our wants as much as possible, the next step is to learn how to handle the anger that inevitably remains.

How does one deal with anger without allowing it to lead to guilt and finally to depression? First it should be realized that many other people are also beset by frustration and its subsequent anger. We must understand that we are not alone in this natural process.

With this acknowledgment, we can realize how other human beings are hungry for delivery from obstacles that bar the meeting of their needs. The superstition that strangers tend to be enemies should be eradicated, to be replaced by the concept that we are all brothers and sisters, all seeking escape from some degree of frustration. But we must also accept the fact that anger continues and will continue to surround us all.

Let us be more specific about anger in that it cannot be completely obliterated. No sooner does one neutralize one anger than another arises. Seeking to dispel anger is therefore a continual battle, a part of life itself. Living in one sense is a struggle without end. However, one who thinks he avoids hostility only deceives himself, because anger that is not handled outwardly is turned inward against the self, resulting in free floating anxiety, emotional stress, and mental illness.

Anger can be dissipated by fighting to satisfy our needs and those of our fellow human beings in order to lessen their own anger, which is often directed against us. The energy provided by anger, its motive power, must be aimed toward the improvement of one's lot and that of others. Mental health is therefore an ongoing process, setting goals toward which one's energy may be directed.

This requires new ways in a changing world that must be evaluated realistically, to be sure that our decisions are not based on superstition of past generations. Learn what is good from the past, yes, but young people must meet needs and aspirations of a more pragmatic nature. The challenge is not only to understand our own psychological makeup, but also to acquire ways of directing anger into channels that will yield more happiness in our existence, in that of our neighbor, and of the world.

CHAPTER VIII

Explosive Hate

It has been observed that repressed anger is suspected as the culprit in a range of disorders from great uneasiness to mental illness. In order to extricate himself from these malfunctions, a person may in desperation seek release in violence. It is as if a boiling liquid in a tightly closed container finally bursts, breaking out of its boundaries. The process partakes of a panic reaction, the only aim being the discharge of long and intolerable tensions.

There is a point in the psychological makeup beyond which no one can go without falling prey to illness. We can stand just so much frustration, and no more, without grave consequences. As electricity accumulated in the sky must at some point yield, so a person under great pressure must find a way to release his tensions.

When that breaking point is reached in the individual or in a group —or even a nation—sanity may paradoxically be saved through violence. This assumption may be questioned in light of the fact that some psychotics are not relieved of their illness although they may be regularly and extremely hostile in a continuous rage. However, such a person's hate is based upon vivid fantasies of persecution that feed upon themselves, replenishing frustration faster than the aggressive energy can be dissipated.

In violence viewed as a safety valve lies the awful possibility that wars, with man's limited ability to express his anger positively, must serve as a tool to save us from a graver situation. The realization of this choice makes one recoil, not because man cannot avoid wars but rather because he seems unable to remove their cause and the basis upon which destructive violence thrives.

Since the end of World War II there have been numerous other wars—some still going on—with their multimillion casualties, suffering, and cruelty. More than 90 million people have been killed in wars in this century, according to a report made to an international congress of the Red Cross.

A soldier in battle represents the repressed hatred of a nation,

58

now suddenly exploding with rationalization of its evil expression. That soldier may be obsessed by a desire to kill and to desecrate. His concern is not with the slogans of politicians and policy-makers back home. His only wish is to annihilate. He has been indoctrinated "to close with the enemy." He despises the world of his adversary, having renounced his humanity for the ecstasy of destruction. The overwhelming urge to kill gives wings to his feet. Rage presses tears to his eyes; it thickens the brain and submerges it in a red fog of hate. And the power to destroy today is more than terrifying. When the first atomic bomb was dropped on Hiroshima, one bomber commander had the power to blast and burn a single city. Today the commander of a submarine equipped with missiles controls the power to level 150 cities, each with several times the destructive force unleashed on Hiroshima.

Wars have long been the crime and the tragedy of mankind. There are always men and women madly in love with death, violence, and destruction. The cruelest, most aggressive, and most ruthless creature man has had to contend with is man himself. But we are at this point not concerned with moral values, but with the cold facts and the bare truth of our existence. We are dealing with and confronting one of the undeniable drives of our beings in groups or nations. This reality cannot be discounted.

The sad truth, according to some sociologists, is that with limited opportunities for creature outlets, wars have served a purpose to release unbearable frustrations. The hatred is directed at a foreign enemy rather than the more practical alleviation of stress existing in a given society.

Without an understanding of the nature of hate and its need for expression, no amount of willful and planned efforts can eliminate wars.

If wars served in the past as a safety valve to drain off the cumulative hatred of a people, then the absence of wars would—if our society remained the same—leave citizens to stew in their juice of bitterness. This is bound to occur if we fail to devise ways to provide the equivalent of warfare or to control the hatred that our society evokes.

We may be reluctant to admit that war might serve a purpose by cleansing hatred on a large scale, thus ironically purging nations for some restoration of emotional equilibrium. Still we have to recognize the evil that resides in the hearts of men. Their aggression must ultimately find expression, if not constructive, then inevitably destructive. Unfortunately, it is the lack of recognition of this fact that makes warfare a necessity until we find an alternative to express our aggressions and hatred in proper channels. In this country, the romanticization of certain types of homicide seems to be part of our national inheritance. We honor the man with a gun; our bandits and gun-slingers are glamorized. The myth of our Western frontiers is built on the image of gun fighters who have set their homicidal tendencies on our culture. In *Crime in America,* a book on juvenile delinquency, Melitta Schmedelberg reports a sad reality: "While millions are spent on advertising soap and cigarettes, only one form of advertisement is free—the advertisement of crime."

This glorification of violent death goes back in our national history. The Minutemen with their rifles are depicted as heroes—as certainly they were. But guns alone did not win the Revolution. We can at least remember Thomas Paine and Thomas Jefferson, whose pens were as mighty as the blasting of guns. But until we stop being fascinated by killing, and as we attain some elements of active self-control and emotional maturity, we are perhaps doomed to wars and meaningless violence.

There is no moratorium in our streets, in cities and towns. We fear terribly the anger that frustration combined with permissiveness has imposed upon our tranquility. If our days are troubled, our nights are filled with foreboding and the threats of thugs, robbers, and rapists who lurk in shadows ready to strike.

Revolutions ironically are rarely initiated by peasants or the deprived people living in ghettos. Nearly always they are aroused and led by intellectuals who would expose the repression of the exploited. They awaken the poor, who tend to see their wretchedness only when it is pointed out by those who view it more clearly.

No nation has produced so much economic goods. Yet even many of the affluent are often in the vanguard of discontent. Obviously, more than comparative wealth is needed to eliminate psychological distress.

We note that violence is exacerbated by the permissiveness that allows repressed anger to emerge, often undisciplined, from the soul of man to outward expression. The anger had always been there. But hitherto it was largely held back by fear, which made some of these people passive and helpless slaves to their neurotic condition.

The nature of permissiveness—freedom to do as one pleases—is ambivalent. Just as hatred can destroy as well as build, in the sense that uncontrolled temper is negative whereas controlled aggression can be positive, so permissiveness also has its baneful as well as its healthy qualities. Experience has taught us that permissiveness aroused by intellectual leaders and the mass media brings to light much that previously had been accepted and borne without protest. The repressed is suddenly revealed and is found to be ugly and repulsive. It awakens a sleeping, obnoxious giant. Now it roams our cities and countryside like a one-eyed monster, with devastation often its only goal.

Permissiveness, like hatred, exists on different levels. It can be denied and repressed. When man is not allowed to assume his own responsibility, there is outwardly a pseudo-peace. The law or the dictator is supreme. No one dares to emerge from the hiding place of his subdued behavior. A well-behaved and submissive citizen is the example of the supposedly civilized man who lives by the rules and never gives his superior reasons to doubt his loyalty. He is well acclimated to the rigors of conformity early in life, sheepishly goes through our educational system, gets a job where he must be a "nice guy" until his retirement, having married and reared a family. All has been laid out like a well-thought-out battle plan. Everything falls into place except the chronic uneasy disharmony and sense of helplessness that subtly and finally disastrously grips his being when he asks, "Who am I? Where am I going? Why am I not happy— why do I brood about my destiny? What is this strange sickness in my soul?"

Permissiveness denied is therefore one road to peaceful existence. No one is expected to "make waves," to disturb the status quo. Our streets are safe again, and authorities rest easily in their homes. It is an ordered, civilized, predictable society, the goal of a favored group for its perpetuation and security. On the other hand, no democracy can really evolve or exist without some limitations on permissiveness. One must not drive against a red light; one must not wantonly destroy property or kill a neighbor.

Some permissiveness allowed, however, is the road to progress, to the removal of injustice. There is rarely an improvement without reasonable discontent and even rebellion against things as they are. This is especially so when the complexities of a society become a labyrinth of incongruities where man may have become lost among machines and inhuman demands. Permissiveness is therefore necessary to open doors to human progress, to extricate oneself from inertia and the threat of a polluted environment.

The anger that is thus released is the price that we must pay. You must allow me to differ, to fight injustice, and to demand improvement in my lot. That is justified permissiveness. It is a request for self-responsibility and the growth of self-identity. The question then becomes how anger is to be expressed. We frankly ask whether we intend to canalize our instinct, to fight in a destructive or constructive manner. That choice of liberated man is the very core of his psychological dilemma. Either he can strike out in a frenzy of illogical and mindless anger in his new freedom, or he can show the trait of an emotionally healthy person by sanely fighting for his welfare and that of his neighbors.

We must accept the fact that no person can exist without some form of justified anger. If this fact, however, leads us to harm indiscriminately the life-support system of our planet—our air, water, soil, vegetation, wildlife, and man himself—it is because we have not yet realized that hatred should be harnessed for the welfare of mankind. The blindness of false values is the villain that prevents us from using our anger for the furtherance of humanity, rather than allowing primitiveness to dominate our hate.

A young man strode to a college podium urging his audience to kill, not specifically saying why, but listing the ingredients of a Molotov cocktail: H_2SO_4, $KCIO_3$, sugar. He explained that if you get a Coke can, pour gunpowder through an opening at the top, add sulfur, steel tubing, nuts and bolts, and then light this combination and hurl it at your target, you thus detonate an improvised grenade. The urge here is to kill impulsively without any prior thinking about the welfare of one's fellowman.

But there is violence in good books, from Mother Goose to Shakespeare. Few volumes depict more violence than the Bible. Even the newspaper that so vividly describes crime and delinquency actually does little more than help bring to consciousness a violence that already exists in the individual. The problem, to reiterate, is not to deny or to repress this hatred, but to find a way whereby it can be utilized for commendable purposes.

It is said that you cannot have the advantages of the free enterprise system without accepting brutalizing mechanization, regimentation by corporate and state hierarchies, degrading environmental levels, and humiliating surplus human beings discarded for lack of skills or for old age, depressing masses of unemployment, welfare, and poverty—all combining to produce the most intense frustrations.

But there is another edge to that sword, that element of destruction in our society. It is becoming increasingly sharp as more and more people awaken to the fact that one's anger can be turned outward against a ruthless apparatus that places profits above human welfare. "We are angry," the consumer advocate dares now to assert. Perhaps recognizing that first step can lead to an even earlier level, namely, the function of excessive frustration.

From distant lands we hear of turmoil as people previously silent now demand the removal of yokes long worn. Not knowing the power of constructive anger, they allow it to be expropriated by leaders whose own anger is directed against those whom they propose to serve. These ruthless people create outside enemies to set up as dummy opponents lest the people see too clearly their own misery at home.

In our own cities, riddled with crime and corruption, mayoralty candidates often employ the same device before an election. The drive for public morality is loud and clear, but it is not against serious crimes that plague the populace; rather it is against prostitution and pornography. Those are always popular issues because only a small minority patronize women for hire. Everything worthwhile, they imply, is free—often even your neighbor's wife. What has the average person to do with these so-called victimless crimes? Most important officials running for well-paying jobs think that an attack against prostitution is sound politically. Without endorsing borderline crime—which, after all, is of little concern to most citizens—why isn't the anger of people directed to more constructive endeavors? Is it not a matter of priority? Is it not more important to provide jobs, to clean up the city, to rid our environment of cancer-causing elements, to take care of the old, to raise the hopes of people, than to arrest a mere girl whose sole means of support is the sale of her body? The man goes free as a participant. The prostitute does not vote, but the customer does.

Today and for many years we shall hear much about the energy shortage, and our President has declared the issue as the equivalent of war. War against what? We have more energy lying dormant in the earth, the sun, and the tides than the nation can use for centuries. Then it is not irrelevant to ask again what war we are asked to wage? Are we ordered once more symbolically to arrest the prostitute as a deflection of our anger? Are we asked to live in cold houses and to shut down some of our factories because acceptable fuels are too expensive? In other words, are private profits so important that the real wants of the people are denied? To what extent are the huge oil companies involved with Middle East sources of supply?

If we support a system of private enterprise—not necessarily monopolies—why must selfish elements predominate? And even if we say yes to this last question, which is our national tradition, is there no way to extract that inexhaustible fund of coal, of oil, of the wind and the sun, and other sources of energy without continuing frustration of our people?

Billions are squandered to arm petty dictators in order that they may slay their own people or attack similar tyrants. We provide guns, planes, tanks, and intricate tools of destruction. We give foreign aid in inestimable amounts, and so many politicians have their hands in the till. Yet if a welfare recipient appropriates a few dollars, he is threatened with jail, and his predicament makes headlines. No one, of course, condones dishonesty in any form—well, practically no one, when we speak of the average citizen. We are speaking again of priorities. We are concerned with contradictions and the frustrations that these evoke, and the resultant anger that smolders ever ready to break into violent hate.

This is the soil that nourishes wars and revolutions, which, given the proper spark, can ignite a fire out of control. A society must lessen frustration if it is to survive as a civilization. On the surface there is much cynicism covering up the deeper anger. We must pray that some demagogue among us does not rise up to harness that anger, to direct it toward unrelenting violence against imaginary enemies.

Of course, not everybody is unhappy. But advocates of reducing frustration aim toward mental health for those who do not possess it. We must be more concerned with the removal of hindrances to welfare. Psychologists in private practice see too much misery to brush it aside. Those who are well can take care of themselves. It is those who cry out against the burden that they bear who must have our attention and sympathy.

A case, as an example, is a boy who upon return from a private school declared his decision not to go back for the next semester. His parents called him a quitter and ordered him to continue his studies there. The newspaper, radio, and television portrayed the result. The boy killed both his parents. After trial he faced the jury without emotion and heard the verdict. But no one asked how long he had withstood other frustrations and unexpressed anger, the depression that had finally driven him to madness.

If people bottle up anger too long as a result of chronic frustration, those who are weakest will be first to break down. Even so a nation that has too long deprived its people of suitable constructive outlets for their anger must ultimately give way to wholesale crime, riots, arson, and perhaps even revolution and war to bleed the hatred out of those who are denied the fulfillment of their rightful needs.

CHAPTER IX

The Criminal

Some people, of course, seek to escape from their problems through direct crime against persons and property, actions clearly defined as being against the law. They pit their cunning and hatred against the establishment and authority figures. It has the elements of a game in which the active participant often loses, adding still greater frustration to compound more and more hatred.

Crime will not be reduced until and unless we see clearly and are well acquainted with our own destructive instinct. The true solution does not lie in the neurotic denial of our own aggression, but rather in the full recognition of our innate and always potential criminality. It is a fact that we may repress this tendency, yet we manage to experience some aggression vicariously through our interest in sensational murder trials and in the daily reports of assault and degeneracies.

Criminal acts are viewed with morbid curiosity as part of the overall package of violence, including automobile accidents and train or airplane wrecks. Within each of us lurk those tendencies that are antisocial and criminal. In the ordinary individual the criminal drives are usually repressed. They generally remain unknown as long as the stress does not become overwhelming.

Criminality is therefore a choice to express in an outward direction the anger that resides in all of us, differing from senseless expression of violence in that the aim is toward selfish satisfaction of physical and psychological needs to the detriment of our fellowman.

The fine line between the action that is specifically criminal and that which is surely an explosive expression of violence is narrowed when planning or intention is blurred, as in riots and arson when people seem impelled by irrationality. This line of demarcation between criminality and uncontrolled violence is more evident in the mass murderer who without reason turns a gun upon anyone who happens to be in sight.

The more there is lack of intention or formulated motive for violence, the more it arises from the subconscious and the deep sickness of the soul. In any case, the problem of crime escapes solution until we recognize its essential nature. Crime, like all other violence, is caused by frustration and the resultant need to express anger outwardly instead of turning it against the self.

Yet the criminal does not always succeed in externalizing his hostility. This is evident in the guilt that frequently follows his crime. This guilt is generally not conscious. Nevertheless, it shows itself in glaring clues so often left to point to the criminal. About 70 percent of those who are sent to jail are repeaters. Apparently there is little effort on their part to evade the law. Legal authorities are constantly amazed at how naive some criminals are in avoiding detection. In fact, the courts have had to institute a series of laws to protect the criminal against himself and his laxness in guarding his rights.

The criminal, according to the frustration-aggression hypothesis, has turned to crime because of the severity of his frustration. In addition, it is possible that his ability to withstand problems is lower than that of the average person. In cases where more than usual frustration is not the sole cause of crime, we may perhaps conclude that genetic and constitutional factors are involved in the inability to withstand disappointments.

The environmentalists, however, still hold that the comparative inability to withstand emotional tension is evolved from bad experiences. The criminal tendencies, they assert, are the result of long and repeated failures of childhood, continuing into adulthood as something that has been taught and engendered by the environment itself.

As early as 1920, Rudolf Pintner said that a person's ancestors are his primary influences, and that the only thing his environment can do is to give him the opportunity to develop the potential with which he was born.

On the other hand, J. E. Watson stressed the primacy of environment. With proper training and education, he said, anyone can become whatever he wants to become, regardless of ancestors.

Even in those years, the two sides were chosen. One claimed that what we are is essentially determined by heredity, by inheritance from parents and more distant relatives. On the other side, scientists asserted that heredity counts for little in shaping what we are, that it is the neighborhood and other environmental factors that steer our development.

Pintner still has his disciples taking his side of the argument, and Watson, too, has his host of followers in our own day.

In *Unraveling of Juvenile Delinquency,* Sheldon and Eleanor Glueck more recently found that delinquents came largely from underprivileged localities, from families that moved again and again, lived in crowded and filthy homes, and existed on the poverty level. Furthermore, the parents of these delinquents tended to be from broken homes, unskilled, periodically unemployed, less educated, handicapped by serious physical problems, mental retardation, emotional disturbances, and criminal records. Abraham A. Santa Clara, in the 18th century, published four versions of the Juda Legend. In one of these is an account of the unhappiness of Juda's parents, a discussion of conjugal infelicity. This was possibly one of the earliest examples of parental discord being proposed as a cause of juvenile delinquency.

Regardless of the argument as to some of the roots of criminality, the fact remains that frustration, the blockage of one's needs and desires, and the resultant anger are the real motive powers of antisocial acts. If, however, lawlessness appears more prevalent in the ghetto, it may be that there is greater frustration there. Perhaps also it is true that these people tend to "blow off steam" more readily than more favored citizens. The corollary to that conclusion may be that those on the upper social and economic levels tend to repress their hostility out of respectability or channel it into business and the professions with a ruthlessness to match the more direct antisocial acts of less fortunate citizens.

The deprivation of unmet needs, especially for belonging and self-respect, make the adolescent gang particularly significant in poor neighborhoods. Youngsters are year in and year out neglected by underequipped parents, leaving them with a feeling of loneliness. Many of these boys and girls also lack opportunities to make their lives meaningful. Without the skills to make their way, the gang becomes a means of meeting some psychological needs for self-identity, while at the same time providing a hedonistic satisfaction in attacking authorities and finding ways to express their hatred.

If bad living conditions and poverty were the only causes of criminality, however, there would be fewer unethical business practices, no bank embezzlement, no petty larceny in plush offices, no stock manipulations or shady methods of juggling accounts.

The fact is that frustration and resultant anger are prevalent among nearly all our population. Criminality takes on many different forms. Shoplifters, for example, are often found to be persons who can well afford to pay for their material needs. The upsurge of crime worries millions of Americans not only in the streets, but also in the luxury of big corporations. Executives and those associated with them can rob others, cheat on their taxes with the guidance of highly paid lawyers, and overcharge on government contracts. And they escape with impunity because of their better education and greater cunning.

Regardless of whether there are more hindrances and drawbacks among the poor than the better off, the fact still remains that our society as a whole provides ever-increasing frustrations, with anger and hatred in all social and economic classes.

A noted criminal lawyer, Edward Bennet Williams, stated, "The criminal justice system in urban America is a shambles and alarmingly close to a breakdown." And yet the courts do favor the rich lawbreaker because he can afford to hire the best legal talent. Generally he stays out of jail on bail, stretching his trial over years by repeated appeals, tinkering with our archaic system of criminal justice.

The affluent and members of some subversive organizations with money from questionable sources both can twist our court system to their best interests. This is so not necessarily because of dishonesty among judges, but rather because clever lawyers take advantage of legal loopholes.

On the other hand, the poverty-ridden criminal, if he is caught, is compelled to accept any lawyer appointed by the court. This lawyer is often inexperienced, uninterested, and incompetent. Our prisons are therefore largely occupied by rejects of society, the poor, the ignorant. They are subject to quick deals by district attorneys to plead guilty to lesser crimes than those that have been committed.

Martin K. Tytell, in *The High Cost of Justice*, wrote, "There are men behind bars in every state who were unjustly convicted simply because they did not have the financial resources to pay the high cost of justice." This situation exists not because lawyers are not available for the poor, but rather because of the current practice of appointing defenders who are ill-qualified or little concerned in cases returning only nominal fees.

Once in jail, the criminal finds himself subject to two policies that are often contradictory: to protect society from the culprit's hostility, and at the same time presumably trying to rehabilitate him for return to usefulness and respectability.

In actuality, the necessity to protect society from the criminal does not require his rehabilitation. All we need do is to shut him in his cell, impose the strictest discipline, and keep him there for the rest of his life. This process of complete isolation of the criminal can certainly be effective, and it serves to satisfy the hatred and vengeance of his victims and of society as a whole. This, of course, concurs with the view that prisons exist to protect others while at the same time meting out deserved punishment.

However, 98 percent of prisoners are returned to civilian life after having served less than three years. The prison, therefore, is not sufficient to protect society, since within a few years the criminal is free to return to his life of crime. The present aim of punishment and isolation for the convicted lawbreaker is therefore largely ineffective. If we must agree that prisons do not protect the public nor punish sufficiently to serve a useful purpose, then jails should exist for other reasons.

It is at this point that some criminologists say that the main purpose, or perhaps the only objective, of imprisonment should be to restore the convict to a socially desirable status. The word rehabilitation is the key one in their vocabulary. They grow enthusiastic over the possibility of changing evil men and women into well-behaved individuals.

Unless we understand the dynamics of the frustration-aggression hypothesis, however, we must struggle in vain with the bad conditions affecting our penal system. If we accept the fact that the mainspring of criminality lies in frustration and an attempt to vent subsequent anger against persons and things, then we must examine our prisons in terms of their tendency to create greater frustrations than those that existed before the crime was committed.

Certainly locking a man in a cell, regimenting him under inhuman rules and regulations, forcing him to wear nondescript clothing, permitting guards to manhandle him, providing him with only nonproductive work, depriving him of mate and children, replacing his identity by a number, and alienating him from society in general —all tend to create immense frustration.

We have succeeded in isolating the criminal from society for a few years, there in prison to develop ever-mounting anger, fed by the very nature of his incarceration. The picture of a snarling beast

behind bars then becomes close to reality. By increasing the hideous-
ness of prison life, we have thus evoked added hatred. Ultimately
it must turn the hardened convict into a monster, later to roam our
streets seeking a still greater vengeance.

However, we have as a nation become increasingly aware of the
hatred generated in our penitentiaries, and as a result have tended to
espouse a more humane approach to the problem. In this connec-
tion the previous faith in retributive vengeance has been weakened,
and recommendations have been made toward lesser punishment,
therapy, and rehabilitation. Many innovations also reject solitude
and penance as effective penal methods, adding our system of
parole and probation to further the humanization of criminals. The
main tendency should continue, not so much to punish an offender as to develop his ability to assume self-responsibility. Liberal
criminologists, therefore, view criminals as suffering from emotional
and social deficiencies.

Unfortunately, permissiveness, more freedom, and a lessening of
cruelty in the prisons may not immediately lower the crime rate. In
order to explain this, one might refer to the example provided by
the growth of permissiveness in the schools. With more leniency,
there has been a proportional increase in problems of discipline.
This is because educators have not recognized that lessening of
restraints allows previously repressed anger to come to the surface
again. The comparative leniency in the courts similarly seems not
to have prevented criminality in the nation. Some people would say
that it has had the opposite effect. This dilemma in our institutions,
as we seek to adapt them to more enlightened avenues, emerges as
one of the difficult problems of our time. Apparently the recognition of the need for more freedom and humane changes is not
enough.

To resolve this seeming contradiction we must reexamine the frustration-aggression hypothesis. Certainly there is plenty of frustration
in prison life even under ideal programs, with subsequent anger and
hostility. With severe discipline, denial, and cruelty there is a repression of overt anger and hatred. It is turned inward, thus keeping prisoners quiet and submissive but like potential time bombs
ready to explode any time.

Some degree of permissiveness, however, releases that anger, as
noted in Chapter VIII. It does not generate new anger so much as
it exposes that which already existed because of many past frustra-

tions. However, the difficulties involved in providing release from primitive and intolerable conditions in penal institutions must not tempt us to take the easy way out by retaining the Babylonian law of retribution, an eye for an eye, a tooth for a tooth. We can no longer afford to stigmatize the average offender as permanently lost and incorrigible. There must be an end to the inhuman atmosphere, an end to sadistic guards whose anger is also engendered by fear and ignorance of human behavior. They, too, are victims of the system, seeking to maintain order where reforms are sorely needed, and getting little outside help. Certainly there must be recognition that an offender should be taught to handle his anger in a constructive manner because authorities in charge will have utilized the knowledge available from the research of social scientists.

If we accept the supposition that frustration breeds anger, and that the aim of imprisonment is rehabilitation rather than vengeance, then our penal intitutions, within the limits imposed for the protection of society, must work toward the elimination of as much frustration as possible.

To expect, however, immediate gratitude and better behavior as a result of enlightened discipline and the elimination of certain restrictive rules is unrealistic and contrary to the principle herein stated. In fact, we should expect the opposite until such time as the penal programs also include channels for the expression of aggression by the prisoners. Ultimately, with that expression will come greater stability and peace. But not before we have organized convicts into a sort of dynamic society to discharge their energies by teaching them how to improve their own lot, by letting them assume more self-responsibility in molding their surroundings and lives.

In addition thus to reducing the prisoner's frustration, there must also be attempts to increase his ability to tolerate whatever frustrations remain for his own protection and that of society. Three factors are necessary, the lowering of frustration, the building up of the prisoner's ability to withstand more of the frustration that will always remain in any civilized group, and finally provision of means and outlets whereby the prisoner can express his aggression in a socially approved manner. This, indeed, is a job for psychologists, good teachers, and others oriented toward the understanding of human nature.

It is true that an effective penal program has yet to be evolved.

Society has not entirely accepted the view that the criminal is a psychological as well as a physical being, with his own need for self-identity and desire for fulfillment like all other human beings.

The public generally defines crime as any behavior that is against the law. Others call an act a crime only if the perpetrator has been found guilty by a court of law. Still others say that criminality is involved in all antisocial acts although they may not be forbidden by law. Furthermore, academic sociologists have their own definition of crime. Accordingly, these varied definitions cloud much of the statistics, with subsequent misinformation or misunderstanding resulting. The confusion thus created enables politically oriented officials to justify those figures that tend to reflect their own self-interest. Data on crime rates in any given locality should therefore be evaluated with some degree of skepticism.

Some psychiatrists believe that criminality is due mainly to neurosis and psychosis, often entirely ignoring the fact that mental illness itself is caused by frustration of essential needs.

Various types of persons are offenders against the law. Some act illegally to extricate themselves from difficult situations. Such offenses include premeditated killing, hit-and-run accidents, and forgery of checks. Another type of offenders is categorized as psychopaths. These people are really rebels without a cause, assaulting and robbing in senseless ways. They act on impulse, inflicting harm and murder for no apparent reason except to yield to viciousness over which they have little control.

In another classification are the professionals who commit property crimes with violence or threat of violence. Blackmail, organized crime of various sorts, and extortion belong in this area. Organized crime is illegally involved in selling services and commodities, including gambling, drugs, pornography, and prostitution. These people also deal in the black market. They sell contraceptives in states where the sale is illegal. They sell tickets to theatrical and athletic events at inflated prices. They smuggle cigarettes from state to state to avoid the sales tax.

Criminal monopoly, an activity common in organized crime, eliminates competition through illegal means. This so-called racket drives others out of business through ruthless action to scare away competitors. Extortion, on the other hand, does not eliminate competitors, but it exacts tribute from otherwise honest business people who can stay in business only after agreeing to pay part of their earnings to the racketeers.

Constituting almost a corporate state, criminal organizations can control large segments of our economy. The theory that poverty is the sole cause of crime certainly can be questioned further in view of the enormous wealth residing in the hands of these organizations. The point reiterated in this book that because of frustrations—frequently suffered in childhood—one may choose to express primal anger in a destructive rather than constructive manner seems to be a more valid conclusion.

Another type of criminal are people in business who break laws applying to restraint of trade, advertising, and other areas. They are rarely arrested by officers in uniform, rarely appear in court, and certainly rarely go to jail. Criminals in these categories are brought before administrative commissions or courts operating under civil or equity jurisdictions. Consequently business people frequently break laws without their offenses being reflected in crime statistics. This bias tends to inflate the record that seems to prove that poor people are more inclined to criminality than those who occupy more favored situations.

So-called white-collar crimes are those of otherwise respectable persons who in the course of their occupation are generally not associated with poverty. They are often suave and cunning, directing their illegal maneuvers in land deals, railways, insurance, banks, stock exchanges, and politics. Even physicians are not infrequently involved in the illegal sale of narcotics, income tax evasion, submission of false reports on accident cases, fee splitting, and restriction of competition.

White-collar crimes do not carry the stigma associated with crimes committed by poor people. The crimes of influential people are diffused in effect and too intricate to be appreciated in details. Yet these infractions of the law are more serious in lowering the moral climate of society, creating a wide distrust in our institutions. These crimes are not as simple as widely publicized robbery or muggings.

Much as we decry violence in the streets and the cruelty of assaults and beatings, still the slow, insidious erosion of our moral fiber created by white-collar crimes does arouse concerted resentment of the establishment in general.

The consequences of this moral decadence include an indifference toward crime. People do not want to get involved, feeling helpless in the overall situation, and faith in the operation of our judicial system is weakened with attitudes that are complacent and often cynical.

One aspect of the criminal justice system is that which concerns capital punishment. Some states already have decided that a person who takes the life of another under certain circumstances should suffer a similar fate. An eye for an eye, a tooth for a tooth is symbolic of capital punishment as a tool of society to redress an unacceptable wrong. Whether or not we agree with that concept, the fact remains that the practice is with us, and that other states are actively seeking legal loopholes to get around the Constitution in order to execute those who kill their fellowmen—except in time of war. The fact is that it is legal and praiseworthy to kill an enemy in battle, but illegal to murder a neighbor—although one is as dead as the other.

Of course we must not equate the blasting of an enemy on the field of battle with the strangling of a helpless old woman by a thug in the South Bronx. Actually, it is not our purpose to discuss the justice or injustice of capital punishment. That question is now being amply debated throughout the land. It is rather our aim to suggest means of permitting a person to die with dignity when the state imposes the death penalty. It is the utmost of indignity and grossness to hang a person or to strap him in a chair either to struggle against electric shock or to suffocate from poison gas. If we are to kill a man, must we also degrade him with a death that is so repulsive, going against all human feelings of consideration? Even the most brutish of men are human beings. There, but for some strange quirk of fate, could be one of us.

This is not necessarily a plea for mercy. It is rather a demand for a more humane way of killing a person if the state has so dictated. If the law insists on capital punishment, we can at least request that the act be more in keeping with a civilized society.

It has been observed that, aside from the psychopathic personality, the criminal usually harbors some element of guilt. How can he make a last atonement for his deed? How can he die feeling that his life has not been entirely in vain?

Instead of snuffing out his life in an undignified and humiliating manner, we could give him a second choice freely allowed by the state.

Today the medical profession is largely limited to experimentation on animals in order to discover new ways of fighting diseases and organic deficiencies. A second choice, instead of deliberate execution, would therefore be for the criminal to offer himself for medical research. Ultimately he would die, but only after his body had been used as a living laboratory for the good of all humanity. What better way is there for giving dignity and a chance to make amends for one who must die anyway?

In one simple decision, the doomed person would largely remove the frustration of having lived a useless life, and also remove some anger against society because it has offered a choice of contributing to the welfare of humanity. His experience will not have been without meaning. There will tend to be no ultimate depression in comparison with the cruelty of being led to the electric chair.

Death will finally be his fate when his body has reached the limits of its usefulness, a painless death induced with drugs to make his last hours without suffering, with the knowledge that people will be grateful for his sacrifice.

This, of course, would not be a way of fighting crime. Aside from removing a killer from society, it would merely allow him to pay for his deed through a procedure that would lend meaning to the termination of a life. There are countless diseases that are beyond the reach of the medical profession unless doctors can experiment on living persons. This in no way is to be compared to the medical atrocities committed under the Hitler regime in Germany, where they were imposed on people who were without guilt. In this case it would involve a free choice to die for a worthwhile cause instead of being ignominiously executed.

Induced death is never pleasant, but what could be more sordid than to watch a man writhing in a repulsive death in the gas chamber? Is it not bad enough that we take a life without any actual and direct benefit to anyone except for the elimination of the criminal from society—and for revenge? We are not quarreling with the right of the state to seek ultimate justice, but we do argue that the condemned man should have the right to determine how he will pay his final debt to his fellowmen.

We can even sympathize with an animal who undergoes experimentation to test cancer-causing ingredients. Certainly dogs and cats do not choose their fate in the laboratories. Animal lovers have long protested against that practice, but it continues because it is the only way now available for the purpose. But what would prevent a condemned person from doing his share for mankind since he was already doomed anyway? The process, of course requiring some changes in our laws, would merely give him a chance to choose his manner of dying, a fate that has already been sealed in any case.

This right would most likely be accepted by many murderers, and it would also tend to lessen the anger of those close to the victim. At the same time, it would meet the need of those who cannot help wishing for punishment. Although the desire for vengeance is not a worthy emotion in a civilized state, nevertheless it does exist. The satisfaction of that doubtful need would be no less satisfied by the sacrifice of the criminal than by the cruder execution in the traditional gas chamber.

CHAPTER X

Targets for Justifiable Anger

America finds itself more divided than at any time since the Civil War. Ethnic groups share the discord of protests and demonstrations in almost all imaginable forms. Even a small group of former mental patients have formed a pressure organization called "Insane Liberation," with a manifesto that makes the startling statement, "We are beginning to see that our so-called sickness is personal rebellion, or an internal revolt against this inhuman society." In other words, the claim is made that mental illness is largely caused by inward pressures imposed by external circumstances. These tensions are built up by frustration and the accompanying anger that is turned inward.

The unhappiness and discontent of America are bursting their safety valves of repression through organizations and rebellious activities of the Black Panthers, through rock and punk music, the communes, Women's Lib, and the partial mobilization of some 13 million welfare recipients. The mood of revolt is stirring even some 20 million Americans over sixty-five years of age.

Television, like a foreboding tide, feeds greater discontent by exposing the sores of our civilization, displaying vacuous people amid empty laughter. Behind the burst of blazing guns and the thud of falling bodies in our entertainment, there emerge the accoutrements of unrealistic luxury and the artificial beauty of the fashion world. All this is deemed within the reach of everyone without effort. The magic and the great expectation are still beyond the reach of millions. Accordingly, the great power of the advertisers manages to create intense frustration in the people, with subsequent anger against mythical figures who would deprive them of all these goodies in the commercials—those healthy girls, the beautiful people, and the throaty roar of sleek automobiles winding through a wonderland of enticing roads that stretch like velvet ribbons.

If the mass media convey much of the glitter of false hope, side by side with the sordid and sadistic, a relativistic morality is not without support and acceptance. A Gallup survey of New York City, for example, shows that about two-thirds of the 1,000 children born to persons on relief every month are born of unmarried parents.

Historian Richard Hofstader asserts that ours is "a democracy in cupidity rather than a democracy of fraternity." Many others say that our system of values has long been archaic, leaving a purely materialistic society with emphasis on property rights rather than personal rights. This contention is based largely on the fact that millions of Americans live at the poverty level—want in the midst of plenty.

Although these critics of the establishment may be reproached with seeing only the wrong side of society, the discussion and division that they create are real enough, arousing even more frustration. Certainly, whatever inadequacies exist among fellow citizens are justifiable targets for anger. Hatred channeled against wrongs is constructive and prevents our hostility from being turned inward against ourselves.

Discord exists not only within the family, but also in most of our social sphere, in many other areas of the community. One would almost conclude that there is a general letdown in means of social control. If young people are angry, there are many outlets for their aggression in fighting the injustices—the fight for good instead of mere destruction. Theirs is the gauntlet; may the young generation use it more wisely than we, the older people, have done.

It is said, also, that we are going through a "crisis in morality," cutting deeply into family life. Ideas of right and wrong are tenuous and shifting in politics, business, law, and religion. It is asserted that any act which is meaningful to oneself is right regardless of its effect on others. The sense of nonaccountability is thus encouraged by people in high places; a new freedom bordering on license is encouraged by authorities at many levels.

The United States is becoming ever more crowded, growing at the rate of 6,400 persons a day. Population growth strains the environment and our natural resources. Pollution chokes the land yearly with 350 million tons of residential and industrial rubbish and sewage—not to mention 15 million tons of scrapped automobiles—all combining to poison the water, land, and air.

We step on each other's toes, and then move on in a great restlessness, ever seeking peace. And instead of emigrating to the countryside, we head for the densely populated metropolis. In the past decade, for example, 11 million Americans moved into trouble-torn cities.

The picture is far from reassuring, with trouble in the streets, bombings, the irrationality of rebels admitting no cause, people locked in their apartments because they fear their neighbors. Children meander with drugged eyes among the ruins of burned buildings. Are these a warning that the time has come to awaken to man's real physical and psychological needs, to acknowledge that hatred cannot forever be uncontrolled when frustrations grow ever more heavy and demanding?

With the rapid changes in our society broadcast by the highly influential mass media, people are confused and bewildered by the many choices open to them. The constant awareness of a multiplicity of choices is an enormous load on the sorting mechanism of the individual. The time comes when the nervous system must cry in desperation "No more" to this problem of choosing, this constant adaptation to places, jobs, and communication. The adaptive machinery breaks down, and shock to the mind sets in.

Over a hundred years ago, Friedrich Nietzsche showed amazingly acute insight into the workings of resentment, the guilt and hostility that accompany repressed emotions. Paul Tillich asserts that Pablo Picasso's painting *Guernica* projects the emptiness and meaninglessness of our society.

When a culture such as ours is caught in the convulsions of a transition period, the individual must suffer emotional upheaval as he finds that the mores and ways that he long cherished no longer provide him with security. Man, largely homeless in the newly emerging culture, is lost unless he can assume added responsibilities, new self-control of his emotions, including his hatreds.

The helplessness of man in times of fear was well illustrated by Blaise Pascal, who commented, "When I consider the brief span of life, swallowed up in eternity before and behind it, the small space that I fill, or even see, engulfed in the infinite immensity of spaces which I know not, and which know not me, I am afraid . . . ."

There is much to fear today in the individual's estrangement from nature, which he has fled to live in apartments that rise skyward but prevent him from seeing the stars. Nietzsche in his day spoke as many others do in our time of the "soul that has gone stale." He said there was "a bad smell—the smell of failure" because many had had their powers blocked. Such failure, he said, was transmitted within the individual into resentment, self-reproach, hostility, and aggression.

Sören Kierkegaard saw the results of this disintegration of character on the emotional life of the individual: the anxiety, estrangement, and loneliness leading to ultimate despair, alienation—having lost his own self-directive and assertive powers. Whenever hatred is turned inward, bad conscience is the result: man's uneasiness with himself, the separation of himself from his fellowman.

People who are full of bottled-up aggression find that whatever they may snatch is purely sedative—frequently drugs and alcohol for promises of emotional oblivion. Ultimately, of course, unless a way is found to externalize the hostility, this in-turned aggression breaks out in sadistic demands or in cruelty out of all proportion to given situations.

Most of our social problems are of urban derivation. Our society is increasingly that of city dwellers. In 1790 a mere 6 percent of our population was urban. Now more than 75 percent live in cities. The influence of the metropolis reaches every cranny of the nation with newspapers, magazines, telephone, radio, television, and superhighways. It is not necessary to experience ghetto after ghetto to feel the pestilence of city life.

The loneliness of urban miasma, the dehumanization, the fear of not belonging, the denial of sharing with one's fellowmen, all reach out through mass distribution of news to enfold with sadness and cynicism the farflung parts of the United States.

The sorrow and the problems are acute in the cities. People are overwhelmed with raucous hubbub to shatter ears and nerves and look up in vain to citadels of steel that shut off the view. Among people packed tightly, curses come easily, but no one hears. Cold and malignant eyes often meet our glances, and no one sees. In the midst of many, there is often that clinging aloneness. In the empty laughter that echoes from the din of pleasure dens and discotheques, there is the silence of the heart and the vacuousness of lost souls, ever seeking some respite from heavy loads.

Social acceptance in the cities is not easily obtained, with few roots of kinship, and real friendship difficult to establish—particularly for new arrivals. Without ties of family and friends, people often tend to act purely for self-interest in superficial contacts. Everywhere one is crowded, pushed in subways, buses, restaurants, sports arenas, and stores. The suffocation of crowds becomes almost

tragic in the late afternoon and early evening when offices and factories disgorge their workers, flooding transportation and roads
leading out of the cities. Expressways become slow-moving park-
ing lots. Short-tempered and bored millions await the comparative
tranquility of home at the end of a long day.

On the road, the automobile serves to isolate the driver from
other people, but one can at least hurl blasphemy at other motorists
and experience bent fenders and sometimes even death as an offset
to the awful monotony. At least while fighting traffic, one can give
vent to hatred. While the air stinks with the exhaust of a million
steel monsters, a driver can curse his fate alone with his tormented
and angry soul. The thousands who die on the highways each year
testify that a potential accident rides beside him in a symbolic death
mask, wickedly and angrily grinning an invitation to senseless violence and disaster.

The easygoing executive or other worker suddenly becomes dis-
courteous, insulting, even vicious toward those who would act as
obnoxiously as he does. Hatred must find an outlet. Here in the
spate of automobiles, each motorist separated from others by an
impersonal elbow distance, with his powerful machine throbbing
at his command—he can indeed let himself go. He can meaninglessly
expel the nastiness that lies within him because of the frustration of
his working hours and finally here on the superhighway.

Blighted areas, slums, characterize much of the large cities, with
evidence of neglect by landlords, politicians, and tenants. In this
fetid atmosphere is bred much sickness and crime. These pits of
deprivation and decadence are an economic liability, not viable in
their self-support, largely subsidized by taxing more fortunate citizens residing in better neighborhoods. The public services such as
police and health departments strain public finance, threatening
the total ability of the city to survive.

In these ghettos are harbored many of the poor, the shiftless and
jobless. Hopelessness flourishes among pawnshops, flophouses, sleazy
burlesques, and prostitutes. Yet slums multiply faster, spreading
their baneful conditions in an ever-widening arc. Landlords of
crumbling tenements often oppose improved housing because it
would deprive them of the opportunity to exploit the poor. And
there are those, of course, who proclaim that the poor have always
been with us, and that in the long run nothing can be done to
ameliorate their lot.

Rage is a condition of life in these decadent areas. It permeates the rubble-strewn streets and the drab and heatless tenements. Anger and hatred blaze in the hooded eyes of youthful gang members and on the features of others at the welfare centers, and in the crowded hospital emergency rooms or clinics where, huddled on rows of benches, they await their turn for endless hours to see a doctor.

The schools are frequently mere detention halls where moody and angry children, rebellious and undisciplined, repeat the meaningless jumble of a society that is not their own. The rage erupts elsewhere in vandalism, in the wrecking of abandoned dwellings, in graffiti like despairing and raucous cries from minds warped by frustration without end.

The problems of the cities are multitudinous. It is obvious that things are not as they should be, that there is a great need for change, for action. A new rationale for social policies awaits those who would siphon their aggression, their hatred of injustice and deprivation, into the solution of these problems. There must be an attack against the complacency and the despair that accept defeat instead of bold confrontation and a fighting back in spite of great odds.

It is not always easy to think constructively, to act in whatever direction is demanded by fairness, to give of oneself toward the betterment of mankind. If men, however, have created the dilemma, men can resolve it by combatting wrongs no matter how difficult and seemingly unyielding. The crusade and the challenges are there. The individual can find his soul, direct his hatred, and taste the joy of self-fulfillment as he battles, ever reaching for goals to alleviate the suffering of fellow humans.

A problem that baffles us with divisiveness lies in the fact that the United States is developing into two distinct societies, one white, the other black, each separated and far from equal. Serious conflicts arise when one group seeks to improve its position or to protect its self-interests. The minority is accused of taking jobs away from whites because they are willing to work for lower wages. In the past, protection for the more privileged group encouraged anti-immigration laws, restricted housing, lack of job opportunities, denial of the right to vote or to hold office, and abhorrence of intermarriage.

It is true that some amelioration has been achieved through enactment of laws demanding fair play for minorities. Laws against intermarriage have been invalidated by the courts, and the trend is toward more equality in employment, housing, and education. But we are still befogged and often against minorities, while at the same time decrying intolerance.

The consequences of racial prejudice and discrimination drain our society of much dynamism and are harmful to the nation as a whole. A poverty-stricken segment lowers the buying power of the economy. The disorders, largely a direct outgrowth of sins against a minority, become a financial burden on all citizens because of the increased need for fire and police protection—as well as other services.

Minority groups tend to react to prejudice and discrimination in one of three ways: they may become overaggressive and violent, they may seek to avoid issues, or they may accept degradation without murmur. The last two methods of adjustment are deemed praiseworthy by many whites. These people hold that blacks should not become involved in controversial issues, that they should know their place and accept the presumption that their race denies them privileges.

Prejudice and discrimination are frequently accompanied by a strange twist of logic that damns the black regardless of his virtue. It is, for example, a virtue for a white person to work long hours, to devote himself arduously to his job. But if a member of a minority group works too hard and too long, it is because of his sweatshop mentality, and—incidentally—it undercuts the white workers with their higher standards.

If a member of the "in" group is competent in business and intelligent, he is deemed to deserve success; however, if a black achieves in the same manner, he is merely cunning and too clever for his own good. The average American is praised for reaching above his lowly beginnings, aspiring upward in his profession, and certainly getting away from manual labor as a means of making a living. But if a member of a minority group resents being compelled to do manual work, he is said to be lazy and parasitic. It would therefore seem that members of the privileged class can change a code of conduct that they consider desirable for themselves into a vice when it is displayed in minorities.

Accordingly, many of those in power accept virtues as virtues as long as these apply to their own activities and attitudes. Many Jews, for example, have attained high positions through intensive study, steady application, and sacrifice. As a consequence, there is a large number of Jewish physicians in proportion to Jews in the total population. Their achievement by prevailing norms should be a matter for praise. Yet, even though there is a shortage of doctors, Jewish physicians are often accused of pushiness, and the non-Jew expresses concern over the possibility that Jews may gain control of the medical profession. Plunket and Gordon state, in *Epidemiology of Mental Illness,* "The anxieties, frustrations, and intergroup conflicts of society since time immemorial have found an outlet in the search of scapegoats and stereotypes."

The people known simply as poor of all races and ages, regardless of origin, are similarly entrapped in preconceived and distorted concepts. Contrary to the general opinion that most of the poor are black, it is a statistical fact that two out of three poor people in the United States are white. Out of 11 million rural poor, about 9 million are not black. The problem of poverty in the richest country in the world presents a paradox of enormous implications.

Side by side with the large number of people living in want is a concentration of economic power so great that it staggers the imagination. The American Telephone and Telegraph Company, for example, derives more income than the three states of California, Pennsylvania, and New York combined. Corporations are burgeoning in size, expanding their immeasurable influence in the economy, becoming giants of financial and political power controlled by an elite management that manipulates more wealth than kings of olden times.

Similarly, in comparison with the ever-increasing numbers of the poor, labor unions backed by billions of dollars press their demands upon the country. Both corporations and unions are groups with highly trained lawyers, public relations experts, advertising genius, and unlimited funds. On the contrary, the millions living in ghettos or on marginal farms have few spokesmen or defenders to press for justice on their behalf.

The country is thus entangled in a paradox. Because so many enjoy a high standard of living, they tend to overlook the physical and spiritual misery that affects the less fortunate. It is evident that for the first time in history we have the means and the power to eliminate poverty, and yet we lack the will to do so. There is little conscience to confront the problem while the poor are largely powerless to improve their lot.

The vision and the aspiration are dim. Yet what area presents a greater challenge, deserving our aggression and even our hatred?

Certainly the fact that we show meager passion and determination to lessen poverty in a nation so rich and powerful as ours should arouse shame and anger.

Many of the old people shuffle in a seedy existence because in their youth they worked for low wages—too small to assure a decent retirement. Complacency blinds us to the helpless elderly as they brood, abandoned, staring vacantly, sickly, awaiting only death. Should not anger arise in an indignation against the wrongs of past circumstances?

Perhaps the poor are also held back by a state of mind. Many of them tend to view life as a tight encirclement, and even the panacea of education does not always encourage them to plan toward a better future. In fact, the idea that education in itself will solve the problems of poverty is not entirely proved. Education bestowed on a person while he still lives in a rat-infested tenement may actually create a greater discontent. There is no simple solution to the entanglement of poverty. It will take all the courage and intelligence of the younger generation to tackle the dilemma from new approaches and with greater dedication.

The tragedy is deepened by the fact that poor people often form a group with its own code of despair in personal chaos—the drunkenness, the tenuous marriages, the unconstrained and misdirected violence almost inevitably linked to a great loneliness.

As a nation we are obviously mired in a complex of problems so intricate, in a network of unending conflicts, that many have thrown up their hands in despair. What are the solutions? There are few solutions, some contend, because no sooner does a partial light appear than another cloud of darkness spreads its pall over the land. Even if we admit that the task is too horrendous for any individual or group to handle, nevertheless it is not so much that we cannot find a solution as that it is a target for constructive anger.

The important factor contributing to mental health is not so much that injustices, crime, and poverty seem insoluble, but rather that one should become active against the obstacles. The frustrations are there, and the anger is there. Must we allow the sequence to proceed toward guilt and its complementary hopelessness and depression? In that direction lie self-doubt, a great uneasiness, and an emptiness. We must reiterate the theme that anger which is not projected outward inevitably becomes deflected against the self.

Our task, therefore, must be not so much to solve problems as to seek their solutions. Many failures may be our lot, but in trying to ameliorate sad conditions, one becomes active, dynamic, allied with the great life force that pulsates throughout the universe. Although we may actually do little for the welfare of others and for our society, nevertheless the mere act of trying accomplishes much for ourselves. A mentally healthy person is active, basically an optimist, because he himself is alive and well emotionally.

As far as the individual is concerned, he may be buffeted by the winds and the tides, but he has within himself the power to feel his own importance in the scheme of things. It is a privilege to fight against discordant elements that surround him. Either he fights or he dies. The important thing is not so much that he must win, but rather that he must struggle, ever continuing that battle as a sign that he is really alive. The exhilaration created by meaningful activities is in sharp contrast to the despair of inaction. A person must move forward if he is not to stand still or even retreat into himself to wither in discouragement.

Fling down the gauntlet of your anger against social wrongs, perhaps to remove some of them, thus lessening frustration for yourself and your neighbors. But even though little success seems to result, still the effect in the end must be to your advantage. Your challenge will expend the energy of your anger automatically instead of allowing it to lie dormant within your own psyche to create emotional distress.

Young people, as well as their elders, should realize that by fighting for improvement of our environment, we reap rewards in better mental health for ourselves. The results are not necessarily public acclaim or appreciation. These are secondary. The rich returns are within those who understand that projecting anger outward against the ills of men and of society is a personal advantage in itself.

The alternative is to sit back in the doldrums of indifference, discouragement, and ultimately despair. The very nature of man is to act even in seemingly impossible situations. A drowning man instinctively reaches even for a straw. His existence demands in the moment not that he change the course of the river, but rather that he struggle to save himself and possibly others near him. As long as he fights, he is alive. If he decided not to pit himself against the current, he would soon be dead—as so many are now dead emotionally because they have refused to confront their lot actively instead of accepting it in defeat.

Early in my career, I concluded incorrectly and too hastily that severely handicapped people were rationalizing when they claimed to be comparatively at peace with themselves. I could not convince myself that a person without hands, or feet, or eyes could function with seeming happiness. After years of observation, the truth became obvious: many of these people were indeed happy. But why?

A good number of handicapped people have struggled and continued to fight against their physical shortcomings. Although they generally knew that they never could become whole again, the reaching out, the never-ending battle to function more effectively gave them a goal, a meaningful extension of their grasp—either with what remained of their bodies or from deeper in their hearts and souls. If their bodies were inadequate, their determination was alive because the anger aroused by frustration had been applied directly to self-improvement instead of being allowed to fester in self-pity.

Accordingly, these brave men and women have a simple but vital lesson to teach. Happiness is within oneself as goals are set, as challenges exist to lighten our beings, as the body and the will take wings with the constructive elements in our society instead of letting hopelessness numb our existence.

The Problem of Emotional Disorders

Mental illness is another puzzling problem in our culture. It is estimated that 10 percent of those now living will, before leaving this world, have to spend some time in a mental institution. These are the people who have chosen or will choose the psychotic or neurotic solution for their tensions.

The neurotic escape presupposes a regression to attitudes held in early childhood. Just as a baby responded to frustration by fantasies —imagining that he was sucking milk from a nipple when actually he was sucking his thumb—some people respond to frustration in the same manner. They seek to solve their problems through imagination rather than by accepting reality. Accordingly, the neurotic has built up imaginary pictures, one superimposed on the other, until he has created a whole emotional structure of fallacies.

The real self, with its capacity for growth, is fighting for its life. It is therefore a conflict between constructive and destructive forces —between the will to fight his environment or to withdraw by turning anger against himself.

When speaking of mental illness, of course, there are various kinds of character disorders, including a long list of maladjustments mainly caused by the inability to handle hostility in a suitable manner. Accordingly, practically all mental illnesses, apart from a few that are constitutionally determined, may be assumed to be based on the ineptness and ignorance that prevent us from handling our emotions properly.

Hate uncontrolled or poorly managed, therefore, may be presumed to be at the root of most mental illnesses. According to Sando Rado, when a person ". . . can neither flee nor fight, he inflicts upon himself the evil which threatens."

Such people are in a state of perpetual anger rooted in situations of frustration; that is, in conditions where urgent needs are not fulfilled and available discharges are not adequate. Thus the anxiety and rage in neurotics represent a disoriented expression of excitation that was aroused by frustration. The anxiety that is so corrosive and almost unbearable is the direct result of being damned up with self-hatred.

The neurotic individual hears the phone ring—it must be something awful. He may be afflicted with physical or glandular disturbances such as dizziness, palpitations, diarrhea, weakness in the knees. He tires easily, is often depressed and listless, and bothered with lack of sleep. Some neurotics become obese or extremely thin. There are numerous sexual difficulties. Victor W. Eisenstein wrote that ". . . a man with unconscious doubts about his potency cannot allay them by making love to the same woman all the time."

Other people suffer from hypertension because they were taught that aggressiveness was bad while at the same time they lived in a world where an enormous amount of aggression was constantly present all around them.

Repressed rage is closely associated with rheumatism, arthritis, and many other kinds of psychosomatic illness such as peptic ulcers and colitis. Phobias affect others with unreasonable fears. There is great anxiety and much suffering in the neurotic with obsessional tendencies, who may be compelled to perform certain acts, or avoid them, or count to a certain number before responding.

The psychotic, who differs from the neurotic in that he has regressed further from reality, is plunged into a cavern of misery where no one seems to hear his cries. Lost in a vast labyrinth of despair, he battles faceless gnomes and giants that torture the victim's soul upon a rack of bewilderment.

The psychotics have left this world for a domain where it is impossible to grasp reality. They can no longer communicate, but must remain alone with their hatreds, which now possess them wholly. Everywhere there are threats and weird voices, scrambled words and strange creatures who wait in the dark corners of their minds to mutilate and devour them.

One might well ask why a given person yields to mental illness in a futile attempt to escape frustration while another manages to bear up under even heavier burdens. Part of the answer must lie in the fact that frustrations differ in kind. A person may be blocked by a stifling or over-demanding environment, by the hindrances of poverty, limited opportunities, and demeaning influences from parents and others. A person may also be severely frustrated by his own personal limitations: inadequate intelligence, negative personality factors, and sickness. There is also perhaps a constitutional index beyond which a person cannot go in his ability to withstand frustration. The so-called threshold of tolerance therefore differs with different people.

One may panic and become disorganized. Another may be constitutionally able to withstand intense disappointment and long-lasting tensions without too great devastation of his personality. For a given individual, however, the heavier the frustration and the longer it continues, the more it will tend to harm him psychologically and perhaps even physically.

The individual's feeling of anger is a warning to indicate that the organism is threatened. The person has been denied the satisfaction of essential needs. Just as pain is a danger signal to indicate that something harmful is afflicting the body, so our response to frustration with anger is merely a sign that something is wrong with the processes in ourselves and in the environment.

Anger, therefore, can be a means of survival, of the ability to exist, to batter one's way into personal stability. That aggression, however, may be expressed without direction, a disoriented outburst of violence. It can be a mere breaking out of tension too long repressed finally erupting with uncontrolled emotion without goal or purpose, giving way at last to tensions no longer bearable. Such overspilling of hatred is always antisocial and in fact detrimental to the person because he is no longer in control but is entirely dominated by the most primitive forces in himself.

On the other hand, the tension resulting from frustration may be expressed in a manner that is socially acceptable in the sense that it furthers social aims and the welfare of one's fellowman. Anger is flung against obstacles that hinder man's progress toward a more humane society, that manacle the freedom and happiness of oneself and of others. Such is righteous anger, released from the mooring of inner self to the environment, molding it nearer to real needs and ideals. It is then guided by a morality based on good rather than evil. Thus are the builders, the mentally healthy, aggressive fighters for bigger dreams and worthwhile goals.

Another way of expressing anger, as we have emphasized, is to drive it within oneself where ultimately it degenerates into self-hatred. This is the way of the mentally ill, of the coward who does not dare fight his environment, and of those who would obstruct justice and deprive brothers of happiness and the right to live.

Fearing retaliation from the world, the neurotic has responded by withdrawing from life's arena, giving up his duties. The punishment for such running away from participation in the healthy expression of anger and hatred is great discomfort. It becomes a suffering that will not let go. But this reluctance to become an active member of groups and society can be overcome if the individual is persuaded again to participate more actively in human affairs, fighting for the good of one's soul and that of mankind, and thus overcoming emotional disorders and the bleakness of existence.

A complicating force has increasingly emerged with tremendous effect on the control of hatred. That is the ever greater tendency toward permissiveness in our society (which has been noted in Chapters VIII and IX). The fight for freedom, for more permissiveness in making decisions and being protected in one's right to differ, to think and speak as one feels—all these have been ideals through the centuries. And now that our society is reluctantly and slowly recognizing the rights of freedom, new problems of hatred have arisen to perplex us with ambivalence and contradiction. Both the good and the bad of freedom are involved in this dilemma. Does the right to freedom warrant muggings, vandalism, and even killings?

First we have noted that permissiveness allows the release of previously repressed anger—in some cases, a good situation. Anything that allows a person to shift hatred from himself into something outside of himself has helped remove one of the main elements of mental illness—although the action may bring even greater harm if the shift is made unwisely.

However, as soon as anger is released from the inner self by permissiveness, then the person must decide how that anger will find an outlet. As we have already pointed out, the person may express it successfully by channeling it for his own good and that of society, or he may express it in a purely destructive manner. On the other hand, the individual may be so frightened and confused by new freedom that he may repress his anger even deeper than before. Thus he may actually exacerbate a previously unhealthy condition, with the permissiveness as the agent of a greater emotional disorder.

When the anger is released by permissiveness, there is a keener awareness of that anger. It is no longer repressed, but stands out exposed to the world. The immediate result is the knowledge that more choices are now available, and the individual is impelled to assume self-responsibility. This situation itself may arouse fear and anxiety. It appears, then, that multiple choices create additional frustration that must be handled in addition to previously existing frustrations. The price of freedom is therefore the necessity to make wise choices—painful as this may be. It is not the antisocial acts that sometimes prevail in the behavior of some young people.

Further complications therefore emerge with the new permissiveness. If now inflated anger is expressed without goal or consideration for others, there may spring up unexpected guilt. In any case, whether the anger is expressed in a destructive manner or constructively, there will most likely be retaliation in response to the confrontation that has been chosen. It is then that guilt or the sense of being "an outsider" may be engendered. On the other hand, the person who chooses a more constructive release will accept without guilt the retaliation that his activities have brought upon him. It will symbolize a good fight worthy of a brave person.

With the dilemma of permissiveness working to complicate his behavior, the person must choose to battle even more strongly and thus himself grow stronger in the process. Or he may choose a return to the false security of repression and a more aggravating character disorder. That decision is the lot of every man, woman, and child. It is the decision to lead an active and constructive life or to withdraw from the world into self-hate and emotional chaos.

We are compelled to acknowledge, however, that many among us are in need of help. The problem confronted by anyone suffering from emotional disorder, or by a person in whose family mental illness appears, is essentially where to find a qualified professional. Since there is much confusion and even quackery in this area, we are impelled to warn of the danger of ignorance in selecting a psychiatrist or psychologist if the need for treatment arises.

The psychiatrist is a medical doctor who presumably has been trained to treat seriously ill people requiring specific remedies, including drugs of various sorts, sometimes in addition to counseling and psychotherapy. The tendency for modern psychiatrists is to depend perhaps too much on pills, shock therapy, and other devices that seem to make little progress in reducing the amount of mental illness in our country. Literally millions of people are in institutions, huddled in special shelters, or walking the streets, drugged into almost perpetual stupor, existing like zombies because the medical profession has largely given up on them.

This book is being written by a psychologist. Obviously he would be better qualified to speak of his own profession rather than that of a medically oriented field. It must be admitted to the layman that there is competition and at times disagreement between the highly trained psychologist and the average physician who takes it upon himself to treat mental illness in which he may have had little instruction in medical school. On the other hand, a really qualified psychiatrist who in addition to his medical training has also undergone a successful analysis of his own psychological hangups to avoid projecting these on his patients is indeed worthy of praise. It is said that a good psychiatrist is worth his weight in gold, and some critics would say that possibly he wishes to collect it all at once, in the sense that a visit may cost from $50 to $100.

Because there are so few properly trained psychiatrists and because of their high fees, it often happens that the average person finds these professionals unavailable.

There is another profession that parallels that of the psychiatrist —with the exception that no drugs or medication are used. We refer to the clinical psychologist who, unlike the physician, studies little of medicine and devotes his education almost wholly to human behavior. Since only a minute quantity of mental illness has organic or physical bases—in which a physician is a must—it would seem that medical knowledge is of little use in treating the mind. However, a good and conscientious clinical psychologist frequently refers patients for medical attention, and increasingly physicians refer patients to clinical psychologists who have knowledge and skills ordinarily not available to the general practitioner or to other specialists in medicine.

Physicians are therefore not so much opposed to clinical psychologists as they are to many other mental health personnel whose lack of training places some of them close to, if not actually in, the area of quackery. They are rightly opposed to unlicensed or noncertified people purporting to cure others of mental illness without the required training. Millions of dollars are paid to charlatans each year by people who are inveigled into the offices of those who are more interested in money than in serving the mentally ill.

Psychologists who have received the required training, including a doctor's degree, a supervised internship, and the passing of examinations, are now certified or licensed in nearly all the states. Their fees are reasonable, covered by major medical insurance and Medicaid. Most of them are listed in the *National Register of Health*

Service Providers in Psychology, obtainable at 1200 17th Street N.W., Washington, D.C. 20036. The register can also be consulted in your local library. It lists psychologists according to geographical locations. There are in addition other directories to guide those who seek competent mental health practitioners. Among these is *The New York State Psychological Association Directory of Clinical Psychologists.* Nearly all other states publish similar guides of qualified psychologists.

There is another national organization for those with specific problems in marriage. Members of that group have similarly met high requirements for private practice, and their names are listed alphabetically as well as by states in the *Register of American Association of Marriage and Family Counselors,* which may be obtained at your local library or at 225 Yale Avenue, Claremont, California 91711.

CHAPTER XII

Doubtful Escapes

Many people have a precarious toehold on reality. They struggle to maintain their equilibrium. Just as walking is a constant effort not to fall, so our sanity is upheld through avoiding the deeper crevices of the subconscious and its primitive adaptation against the stress of living. In the back wards of mental institutions are the despairing cries of those who have lost their way, those who can no longer distinguish the difference between the real and the fantasies.

Awakening in a strange room, an ordinary person may be bewildered for a moment, with sleep still clinging to his being—dazed and hanging in some sort of unreality. Eternity stretches before and after. In between, the person struggles for a brief moment of nothingness and indecision until he catches a familiar object, feels the beating of his heart. "I am here—I am real." And as suddenly he awakens to reality, having regained identity and the locus of his existence. In sleep we wander unhindered in our dreams, oblivious to chaos except when nightmares plunge us deeper into that inner self.

That strangeness lies sometimes barely beneath the surface, ever ready to emerge. We utilize various devices to ward off the threat within us—the anger that often lurks in the secret recesses of the mind.

A person is not necessarily depersonalized by viewing himself as an energy system—in that, for example, the energy generated by hate cannot be dissipated without some expression of it. Rather, man's alienation comes as a result of the frustrating of the normal expression of that system. It is only then that he experiences himself as an automaton, or robot.

A state of mental misery is generally due to failure of adjustment resulting in loss of contact with reality. It is inability to handle one's emotions. It comes from misdirected action with final abrogation of self-responsibility because of repeated surrender to irrationality. It is a voice without hope of being heard, a loss of identity, alone except for irrational or repressed anger.

Like the Spartan youth with the stolen fox eating into his belly, he who is the victim of the great discontent cannot really admit his pain because the world would not understand or does not want to understand.

It is the nature of the human animal that he must satisfy his physical and psychological needs in order to survive. Frustrated in these needs, he must struggle, as he has from time immemorial, to overcome the obstacles that bar his way.

We spend over half a million dollars a year just to put ourselves to sleep, or to stun ourselves into a stupor in order to get away from the consciousness of our surroundings and to ease the sickness within us. Over 800,000 pounds of barbiturates are produced each year. But that is only one kind of numbing drug to deaden our nerves and emotions. There are more than 200 other types of sleep potions also available for the person who would prefer to sink into dreamless numbness and escape.

More than half of the drivers on the road are under the influence of drugs—antihistamines, tranquilizers, hypnotics, and antispasmodic drugs, sedatives, amphetamines, and antibotics.

A person on LSD will see and hear things worse than those he seeks to avoid. The heroin user will be grateful for the stupor that comes upon him—even the final exit that leaves him huddled hideously on the living-room floor. Marijuana has become fashionable, frequently served with the aplomb of the gracious hostess.

Man's moods are subject to an ever-changing pattern or spectrum. Influenced by inner and outer experiences, a person's ego moves back and forth across this spectrum. At one end lies melancholia or depression, at the other end, mania or extreme agitation. The well-balanced person tends to linger in the middle range, only rarely going to extremes. If and when, however, he does experience an unusual emotional response, his psychological, endocrine, and other biochemical elements adjust themselves, and harmony is restored. In the person afflicted with emotional sickness this adjustment does not occur. The over-agitated individual at one end of the spectrum is nervous and anxious. His tension will respond to drugs that soothe and tranquilize; the person at the opposite end with his heavy load of depression can hardly raise his head. His life is empty, without meaning or happiness. He will respond, however, to a mood elevator—for temporary relief, needing more and more drugs to enslave him as the price of his escape.

Yet many who seek withdrawal from narcotics must go through untold agonies, even banging their heads against the wall just to feel a more human and normal kind of pain. A person's teeth loosen, perspiration pours over his body; he vomits and defecates endlessly. Muscles cramp and tighten until they seem like solid rock, while cold chills rack the whole body alternating with burning fever.

Others seek to flee from themselves at the dinner table, over-eating, underexercising, growing obese, and subsequently striving for what they have lost—a slim and graceful figure. The neurosis that made them compulsive eaters now impels them on to another pseudo-self, the slim idols of the movie screen and television make-believe. Cookbooks side by side with diet books are best sellers, and finally in desperation the fat person turns to the medical profession to ameliorate his condition.

Drugs generally used for weight control include sex hormones, barbiturates, amphetamines, laxatives, and diuretics as well as thyroid and digitalis—all drugs which in small quantity do not work in reducing weight, or if they do work are definitely not safe according to authoritative medical sources. And yet, as if conniving in the vain attempt of people to escape from themselves, there are 5,000 to 7,000 doctors who until recently saw as many as 10 million patients who consumed 2 billion diet pills, grossing for these unscrupulous doctors a billion dollars a year. There are always those in any profession who are ready to profit at the expense of people caught in the clutches of their own great discontent.

To evade inner torment, others turn elsewhere. They, as alluded to in Chapter I, beat a retreat from distress by becoming addicted to alcohol. Married middle-aged women of middle and upper classes have become an increasingly larger percentage of the alcoholics in this country, according to the National Institute of Mental Health; and people of both sexes who shun their anguish through alcohol increase at the rate of 200,000 new cases each year.

And so various means of alleviating the tension—in a sense, an escape from anger—are utilized. Among these none is more prevalent than the reckless driving of automobiles, as also mentioned in Chapter I. The millions of machines roaring on our highways not only create added stress, but also serve to express the hatred, the anxieties that afflict individuals. The automobile is a symbol of power, of mastery, of destruction as well as a vehicle for covering distances, a device that almost sets us free from space and presumably from inner torments. It is the magic carpet that sweeps us onward from ourselves into fantasies of vindictive achievement and killing. The negligence, the recklessness, and the ruthless discourtesy as well as the abundance of risk-taking bespeak the hate that dominates many drivers, as they seek both to express hostility and to break loose from its accompanying hurt.

The first and essential step of prevention, according to traffic experts, is the awakening of the public from apathy. As if those who are responsible for 50 percent of such accidents—the alcoholics who form only 4 percent of the drivers—could be scared by the horror of these accidents. In fact, the recitals of gory details, the pictorial presentation of mutilated bodies, and other methods used presumably to frighten those who endanger lives on the highways may actually encourage more such accidents. After a six-month anti-smoking campaign, for example, a survey by the Ontario Medical Association showed high school students smoking more instead of less in spite of the serious harm depicted and described.

If most accidents are caused by hatred expressed destructively, then a greater awareness of the horror of automobile accidents may merely invite greater recklessness. If we add to this desire for hostile aggression a sense of guilt that becomes translated into the urge for self-destruction, the motives for highway slaughter emerge.

A study of "uncontrollable violent behavior" as the cause of many automobile crashes was suggested by an advisory committee to the Secretary of Health, Education, and Welfare. Part of this report on traffic safety said, "It may be that the popular conviction that automobile accidents are the fault of drivers arises from the perception of aggressive behavior on the part of others—and oneself—in situations where it is clearly intended."

In 1895 there were only four gasoline-powered vehicles in the country. Two of these in St. Louis managed to collide, injuring both drivers. "Thus," the report commented, "was introduced a form of pathology that was to grow steadily from that year to this." The present-day annual number of deaths and permanent injuries is tangible evidence of man's hatred and his attempt to run away from it.

Many accidents are therefore the result of ignorance, the consequence of suppression that incidentally attributes evil to all aggression. Those who are most prone to accidents display an explosive type of hatred—too long held in check—which marks them as persons angry at the world. Excessive drinking of alcohol, of course, serves as a weakening agent that allows the destructive tendencies to emerge and to become a menace to other drivers. It has been reported that emotional disturbances are the cause of at least 75 percent of all accidents. Thus the accident causers are generally full of frustration, anxiety, and a sense of inferiority because in the past their hostility has been effectively blocked. The frustration and anxiety associated with the onset of adulthood in the age range sixteen to twenty-four accounts for the greatest percentage of accidents among these young people.

However, a person not only seeks to ameliorate the inner tensions and the hostility by so-called accidents; he also tries to free himself from the pangs of hate by various other avenues similarly self-defeating. It is understandable enough how drugs, excessive smoking, compulsive eating, and the consumption of alcohol all can serve the purpose of destroying the self. However, it may be less obvious that sex can also be directed to the same goal. Clinton T. Duffy, former San Quentin warden, for example, claimed that 90 percent of the men in the nation's prisons are there because they have had or still have sex problems. Whether or not we agree with that conclusion, the fact remains that sexual difficulties are at the root of much frustration. There is a vast amount of literature depicting the tortuous ways the sex drive seeks to meet neurotic aims. Walter Kaufmann in a book on existentialism which he edited reports, for example, that "Cleopatra—was fond of sticking pins into her slave-girls' breasts and derived gratification from their screams and writhing."

In this country, we have the highest incidence of sex crimes in the world. However, it is erroneous to assume that sexual disorders occur mostly among demented persons who stalk dark alleys and the cells of our prisons. Our high divorce rate perhaps indicates that great sexual frustration exists in many marriages that may have appeared on the surface to be harmonious and stable.

A sense of inadequacy is generally present in the person with sexual problems. Whether or not we agree that this feeling is a remnant of childhood trauma, we cannot deny that the adulterer is moved by dissatisfaction with his present relationship and his mate. It is true that the strength of the sexual drive differs greatly among individuals; but it is also true that promiscuity may be based upon a need to prove onself—to affirm one's masculinity or femininity. It has been estimated that 60 percent of married men and 35 to 40 percent of married women engage in extramarital sex.

The sexual act may be sadistic, an attack upon a mate, as the child originally viewed such an activity; or it may be masochistic— a sense of being attacked and mutilated. People whose minds have been tainted by such neurotic distortions are never satisfied with sexual relations, having been robbed of the self-realization that real love union permits. Going from one partner to another, they are forever seeking release from an inner anger that they seek to express through their sexual activities.

There are other ways of evading the anxiety aroused by repressed anger, including the concentration upon the opposite of the offensive impulse. For example, as noted in Chapter III, if a person feels hatred for someone else, he may in self-defense love him. Love then becomes a mask for hatred. Love for a dominating parent or guardian is frequently of that nature. When the authority figure falls from power, the hatred can then emerge with great suddenness and may be reflected against all authority figures. Former heroes become "pigs" and strutting militarists.

Some people, of course, never grow up; they remain emotionally fixated to a childhood stage of development. Again it seemed safer not to mature, not to assume responsibilities. There are four stages in our growth, both physical and emotional: infancy, childhood, adolescence, and adulthood. Normally a person passes from one stage to another with fairly steady progress. Sometimes, however, a person halts at a given stage, remaining fixated psychologically, and his emotional growth is said to be stunted. Such a person is afraid of going ahead because he fears what may be forthcoming.

What does the fixated person fear? What dangers hinder the forward thrust of his progress? The chief threat is the anger of others, of parents, of other powerful figures who prevent him from expressing his own anger. He feels incapable of handling his hostility or doubts its effectiveness. It is less dangerous to remain inadequate and fixated to childhood or even infantile ways of doing things. Just as he once suffered from separation anxiety, fearing to leave the mother or the protective shelter of the home, so in adult life it becomes habitual to seek safety first rather than venturesome endeavors.

The child who is overly attached to his mother is held more by fear than by love. He may thereafter be dominated by that fear and thus continue to avoid confronting his hostility by withdrawal into submissive or passive behavior.

Others may progress in their ability to handle their hostilities and thus take the succeeding steps on the ladder of their psychological development. Having tentatively acquired maturity, suddenly a catastrophe or a series of frustrations may overtake them. They then seek to escape from themselves by regressing to an earlier stage, becoming childlike again as a means of avoiding the anxiety evoked by their unacceptable anger. A young woman who becomes angry in a quarrel with her husband returns to the security of her parents' home. One who has suffered from the world's strife may withdraw into private fantasies. Any flight from realistic thinking becomes a regression. Vandalism, for example, is in the nature of such regression in that the child returns to an earlier and irrational way of expressing hostility.

On the other hand, to obtain some degree of release from inner pressures, the anger may be channeled against the body itself, that is, the physical being. This is the nature of psychosomatic illness. It is an assault on one's physical apparatus as an outlet for intolerable frustration. Although psychosomatic illnesses, such as psoriasis and many other disabilities, have their origin in the mind, these illnesses are real enough, according to information from the Duke University Medical Center, Division of Psychosomatic Medicine.

Many people are not willing to accept the fact that emotions and stressful situations can play a large part in causing physical illness. Yet such mind-body phrases as "You make me sick" and "He gives me a pain" show that unconsciously people recognize that strong emotions and frustrations can be reflected in physical disease. Everybody has some deficiency somewhere within the organic inheritance. This weakness may be in the gastrointestinal tract, the cardiovascular system, or the urogenital system. It follows most often that repressed hate and its accompanying conflicts become localized in one of these systems in the form of disease. Latent rage takes the form of change in physical function and eventually in tissue alterations.

People most susceptible to psychosomatic afflictions generally lack the belligerent attitude suitable to their well-being. They do not possess the natural self-assertion necessary for mental health. Just as unused muscles must atrophy, so do aggressive impulses if not utilized. Finally when an emergency does occur for the assertion of self, the person finds that his ability to act is no longer at his command. Long repressed, the ability to be angry has finally been totally blocked as far as its overt expression is concerned. The person's ability to fight back, however, has turned upon himself, where it may actually eat into his organs and tissues. Generally a person who is most apt to develop psychosomatic illnesses is one who has early identified himself with a very strict person in his childhood, and later with the standards of society. He is indeed a law-abiding citizen. He has few opinions of his own. His highest values may be cleanliness, order, decency, and punctuality. As far as others are concerned, he seems to be functioning satisfactorily, rarely getting into difficulty in interpersonal relationships because although he fails to stimulate, he is industrious, very exact, and in some cases quite ambitious and anxious to get on in life without dishonesty or disturbing the status quo and the comfort of others.

Many try to exorcise unhappiness through the high priests of our secular society: psychiatrists, psychologists, guidance or marriage counselors, not to mention the out-and-out quacks in mental and emotional manipulations.

Living in an increasingly automated industrial-urban society makes millions of people strangers to themselves and to their deepest needs. In response to this situation, a vast number of so-called mental health workers have emerged with a variety of methods and schools. Our newspapers carry their advice, their recommendations for curing a broken heart or a backache. Their lofty pronouncement presumably is deemed necessary for one in four adults who thinks that he has emotional problems serious enough to call for professional assistance. Television and radio are no less active in purveying their cure-alls for character and social disorders.

No less than 36 separate schools of psychotherapy offer their wares. Styles in psychotherapy come and go. Some years ago, Freud and psychoanalysis were supreme. Now we are told he is no longer in fashion, even though all systems that attempt to delve into the deeper part of the personality are directly indebted to Freud.

More widely accepted today, however, are the Jungian aim at integrating the personality, the Adlerian goal of changing one's lifestyle through greater subjective and social awareness, and the Harry Stack Sullivan approach, which seeks genuineness and immediacy of

104   *Coping with Anger*

interpersonal experience. And Fromm is concerned, too, with the aims of other schools, but assumes that these goals must be attained within the framework of a sick society.

Differences in techniques and goals among those who presume to alleviate our mental and emotional discomforts are multitudinous. Differences exist in the focus of inquiry, the relative importance of past and current situations and therapeutic goals. It would almost seem that there are as many kinds of psychotherapy as there are those who do psychological and psychiatric work.

These mental healers come under a variety of names and classifications. Their shingles invite the weary, the alienated, those whose suffering is in the soul and mind more than in the body. Their fields extend to psychoanalysis, psychobiology, psychiatric interviewing, casework, psychologic counseling, and many other areas.

If in his misery a person decides to get professional help, he may well be confounded by this wide variety of types of therapy. Should he seek a therapist such as Adolf Meyer or one of his disciples who practice "common sense" therapy? Or should he try psychoanalysis? What about the followers of Adler, Stekel, Jung, Rank, Horney, or Sullivan? Perhaps hypnosis, narcosynthesis, or short-term therapy as practiced by Alexander and French? There are also nondirective therapy according to Rogers, or psychodrama as advocated by Moreno. Of course you could choose group therapy, organ therapy, or perhaps "conditioned reflex therapy."

The highest in this priesthood are the psychiatrists—the medically trained psychotherapists. And yet even these differ in their methods and aims. Two psychiatrists, for example, trained in the same manner in the same school, with similar medical background, each will handle therapeutic problems in his unique way. It is said that there are no sciences in psychiatry, merely opinions.

It is disturbing for the average person to consider the multiform methods of treatment that are used against emotional illnesses. We listen to the claims of their devotees and to the acrimonious criticism of one another. And yet it has been repeatedly shown that no one method of professional personnel is superior to any other. How can the average person who needs psychological help work his way out of this maze of uncertainty.

That question has been answered very specifically in the previous chapter. It cannot be emphasized too strongly that the public must be protected by the necessity to seek out professionals whose competency has been vouched for by a State Board of Examiners and who have thus been licensed or certified. That license is supposed to be on display in the office of the psychologist or marriage counselor. Even then, psychologists differ in their professional skills just as State Board–certified surgeons differ in theirs. However, the chances taken in any health field are certainly reduced when one's choice is limited by the licensing of those who for a fee offer their services to those seeking help for emotional problems.

CHAPTER XIII

Resolving the Dilemma

Our present aim must be the consideration of a program, a set of attitudes and specific directions on how to accomplish our purposes. This problem will include a scale of values to help guide and judge one's action, ways of handling frustrations and anger. Accordingly, the person can cleanse his soul of hypocrisy and sham for truth and honesty. He must cease a parasitic existence with the assumption that others can solve his problems, that the world owes him a living and solutions. Salvation lies in each within himself; in spite of many obstacles each must find his own way, his own course of liberating action. And until that condition is accepted, a mirage of hope must always be tomorrow, in fantasies and ultimately in disappointment.

First it should be reemphasized that all instincts are divided into two main categories, those moving toward life and those inclining toward death. The death instinct is considered a primary force in all living things. It seeks the return to a state of inertia, rest, and ultimately death. This negative force is opposed by the life instinct, which constantly attempts to extend life and to aggrandize it toward ever higher unities. Examples of this are the urge to procreate through sexual activities and the tendency to fight for self-preservation. There is also a second interference with the death instinct external to the person in some segments of society, which strives to protect members of the group with rules applicable to all—such as taboos against incest or murder.

All nature is hostage to these two forces, working with unrelenting impulse to be born and finally to die. Plants and all the vegetation that supports life are likewise first seeds to sprout into fruition, only in the end to return again to the soil.

All our activities tend either toward death or toward greater life. It seems that this is the perpetual choice of man. Either he lives or he dies. But while living, he can live to the fullest, constantly lending his hand to the life instinct, knowing all along that there is a vast reservoir of energy in nature to propel him onward. He can dare to move rather than to stop, putting off the final escape into mental illness or postponing death. He must set aside hopelessness and passivity, prevent being overwhelmed by his environment. He must join hands with the life instinct and cease to be fascinated and lured to his own self-destruction.

To live is to act, to move, to be a part of vast conceptions and adventures. To die is to cease one's action, to become inert and directionless. The life characteristics of greatest importance include a tendency toward doing things and the inclination to relieve anxiety through action.

Action toward what? The person must be guided by norms—or else any kind of violence would be considered on the side of goodness. A person must therefore seek the expression of his hostility and aggression toward specific and worthwhile goals or else he could as well find expression for his hatred through crime or other antisocial maneuvers. Dangerous human proclivities can be canalized into comparatively harmless courses by the existence of opportunities for self-improvement and for the good of society.

Young people must then ultimately fall back on the age-old questions. What is good and what is evil? What are the criteria that should guide one's direction? What action is wise or unwise? How does man harness his own powers in unison with the life instinct? These questions have occupied philosophers through centuries. Yet at some point, if the person is to have real meaning in his existence, there must come a concept as to the locus where he stands in this life. Only then can he, according to his own judgment, evaluate his days as productive or sterile.

Three kinds of motives determine the nature of a person's conduct: (1) pure self-interest; (2) pure selfless interest in others; and (3) an interest that is a synthesis both of self-interest and interest in others.

According to the pure self-interest point of view, the true motive of all our conduct is essentially selfish. All hedonists—those concerned only with themselves—believe that self-interest is the one motive that dominates all human conduct. We are told that egoism is natural and therefore right. That philosophy, it is contended, conforms to the impulse of self-preservation. Each person must will his own welfare for himself. An individual therefore must attend strictly to that part of humanity over which he has direct voluntary control, namely himself. By taking care of oneself, the highest welfare of humanity is thus achieved. If, in fact, we desire the welfare of others, let us forget about them and attend to our own needs.

The opposite view, of course, is pure selfless interest in others —absolute altruism. According to that philosophy, the true motive of conduct is devotion to the welfare of others in utter disregard of oneself. One should never think of his own self-interest, but always of the interest of others. Only in this way may the highest welfare of humanity be attained.

The interest that is a synthesis of self-interest and that of others, however, affirms that the true motive of conduct lies midway between the two extremes of absolute egoism and absolute altruism. This is both egoistic and altruistic. It sanctifies or develops self and thus is egoistic. But it sanctifies the self also for the sake of others. The development and satisfaction of the self both as an end in itself and as a means of helping others is the essence of the ego-altruistic motive of conduct.

This dualism in purpose links the person with universal trends, makes him in tune with his fellowman. He is no longer alone, but rather synchronized with higher aims than himself while at the same time not abrogating the responsibilities he owes to the self.

Whenever the individual thinks of both himself and others in regulating his conduct, he sets in motion a balance between himself and the outside world. An equilibrium is established, a sort of rhythm tied to nature itself.

If man acts purely for his selfish interest, the balance is skewed in favor of isolation, a loss of contact with others. Being egocentric, he tends increasingly to be alone. He may win many battles, but ultimately he must lose the war against the negative forces in his environment. The balance is heavily weighted with himself while the rest of the world hangs precariously in the air with little significance for the self-centered individual. There is no longer any rhythm to his life; he may have gathered much unto himself, but in the process he has lost his humanity, the ability to feel and to touch other beings. His loneliness must finally tip the scale into hatred or self-destruction. He has become permanently separated from the source of all real inspiration—the approval of others; and he lies in disharmony with himself and with nature.

If, on the other hand, his concern is purely with the welfare of others to the exclusion of his own self-interest, the person similarly has detached himself from real communication with others. Neglecting himself, he proves incapable of helping the world. The link between two parts is destroyed because in losing himself the person cannot long continue to establish empathy with others.

In order to be effective in promoting human welfare, more than an altruistic motive is required. The doer must be capable of doing. One of his responsibilities must be to develop his own capabilities and potential. A weakling cannot be effective in solving the problems of people, of the community, or of the country.

We are told that the individual must start with himself, then attempt to improve his immediate surroundings, help other people, and finally extend efforts further outward until his consciousness embraces the world.

Without espousing the pure self-interest approach or the completely altruistic one, the individual must also be concerned with himself—his physical and psychological needs while at the same time the needs of others are merged with his own.

The problem of concern to anyone functioning in our society must be a reduction in the amount of frustration that acts upon him. If therefore the person is to improve his chances of survival in our automated and technological complex, he must find ways to remove as much of the frustration as possible. This he will achieve largely by assuming that he can increasingly meet his own psychological needs, while not neglecting the needs of others. Let us clarify further the personal and psychological needs that should be met if one is to reach his full potentialities. These needs have already been touched upon when we discussed their emergence in childhood. As an adult you must assume the responsibility to fulfill your needs, actually to wrest them from the environment. Cameron and Margaret in *Behavior Pathology* wrote: "Let us then define need as a condition of unstable or disturbed equilibrium in an organism's behavior, appearing typically as increased or protracted activity and tension."

The person has to be involved—becoming one with others, belonging to groups that will help him develop his abilities. Negative forces tend to make us withdraw from activities. Man can only find himself through his fellow human beings. The life instinct urges us into belonging, the opposite of isolation. The species could not have survived without mutual help.

However, self-realization can come only through merging with others. Not only business contacts, but simply contacts for the mere expression of oneself. Man cannot function in a vacuum. He must dare to operate with his neighbors—thus accomplishing two purposes, providing an outlet for his talents and the emergence of his feelings for others while at the same time participating in helping those who similarly need human contacts for their own happiness. It is a give and take, a sharing on one's emotions and ideas, and the opposite of alienation. Man is not strong enough to get along without cooperating with his neighbors. Harry Stack Sullivan rightly concluded that ". . . the self is the product of interpersonal relations." This does not mean that one must be subservient to others. It does, however, imply that one's own welfare is inextricably linked with that of others.

One must dare to act, to be active. Erich Fromm expressed the same thought, saying, "Happiness, which is man's aim, is the result of 'activity' and 'use'; it is not a quiescent possession or state of mind." Inertia is death, action is life, the pulsing forward of one's psyche into human relationships that enrich and invigorate. Belonging to groups is one of the greatest needs of the individual. Sharing one's aspirations, hopes, and dreams is a means of expressing one's humanity, functioning as a warm and sympathetic person rather than as a distant and suspicious character. It is only by giving that we may in turn receive. Happiness lies in reciprocal arrangements whereby one shares in empathetic interchange the spirit and the goals of common good. The walls of pure self-interest without appreciating the needs of others keep a person from self-realization and self-growth. Man is never sufficient unto himself, and only by reaching out toward those who surround him may he reap a richer harvest of personal satisfaction. It is not hypocrisy to note and to express appreciation, and by thus bolstering the confidence of others we, too, may in return receive goodwill and friendship.

This friendship is not something that comes without our effort, but it is an active reaching out to share, to give, and to receive. It is something that we must deserve and earn—and only those of short vision expect it without conscious effort on their part. The greatest curse that can come to man is to feel permanently alone; and that he may bring upon himself by refusing to use his talent to share with others, to help alleviate their sorrows, and to lend a hand toward their happiness. Denied of this need for love and affection, a person must as a consequence become a victim of hate, drawing the same conclusion as Richard III, who with pitiless self-cruelty enumerated his failings and decided that since he could not be a lover, he must determine to be a villain.

Another psychological need of everyone, which if met tends to reduce frustration, concerns achievement. No one feels more helpless and useless than the person who is not doing something worthwhile. Work is not necessarily achievement; it may be merely defensive to avoid poverty, insecurity. Most people work, but few really achieve, or get a feeling of inner satisfaction from creative use of their environment. Work has frequently become drudgery, dissociated from pleasure or individual initiative, monotonous with few tangible results. Yesterday's tasks today have been merged and integrated into those of many other employees so that the end product belongs to everybody and to no one in particular. The specialization of technology has flooded us with economic goods and largely denied man of the need to achieve. Work, therefore, is not infrequently a means of increasing frustration rather than decreasing it.

This process must be reversed, with the person actively planning ways of mating work with his own interest and welfare. To waste life in work that brings boredom rather than pleasure is the tragedy of too many. The person certainly has only one life to live—and to live it negatively, as an automaton with seemingly endless monotony, is the curse of those with little courage, the cowardice that binds man to pain and destruction of spirit. If this is the price of economic security, then perhaps the price is too high. A comparatively free existence has a greater value. Work that is creative and soul-satisfying is the greatest boon granted an individual. Almost any action is worthy of execution if it liberates one from drudgery.

Economic security is relative. A man gives up a high income to wrest his living from a rock-ribbed farm and enjoys a happiness given to few. The greatest deception in our civilization is the compulsive urge to accumulate things. We are surrounded with cars, expensive homes, club membership with its prestigious demands, its show of affluence—and yet love, sleep, the pleasure of using one's body, the eating of simple foods, and the thousand other ordinary pleasures all are easily obtained without the competition of pseudo-wealth in dollars and cents. And yet meaningful work itself should be a cure—and in fact it is a deterrent against unhappiness. This is so evident upon retirement. Physical and mental illness too often engulf the senior citizen. A person should never actually be unemployed as long as he is physically able to work—even if it means doing tasks of a purely voluntary nature. There is work for everybody if he is willing not be tied to a regular job. There is need for volunteers in a thousand and one places—in hospitals, in politics, education, religion, and charity drives. There are gardens to be dug, homes to be improved, and help to be provided for less fortunate neighbors. The world is crying for help, and yet some of us complain that we have nothing to do. Life without work is often a struggle against demoralization and anomie.

Of course, one has to face the fact that there is a need for the basic elements to keep alive. We are assuming, however, that many people possess these necessities, that the curse of our civilization is that we expect too much as a neurotic drive rather than as an urge merely to express oneself. Contrariwise, if economic goods are sought essentially as secondary and not as a compulsion hiding deep-seated conflicts, then such striving is not harmful. It is, as is usual, when the job and the chasing of the dollar become a hectic, meaningless and nerve-wracking race that man becomes automated, alienated, and lost. That is when a man must act to save his soul and his sanity—because his world is bound to fall apart at some point, with the wreckage of his life scattered in ultimate failure, in poor health, and other disasters. Man must dare to be free, dare to pay the price for his salvation, find at last work that is a balm to his soul rather than a curse, or blackness without end or meaning.

For those who cannot escape the daily grind, frequently with corrosive meaninglessness, there are still hobbies to be pursued, a second job, creative outlets in arts or crafts. If man is to find self-realization, he must complete things. In *The Stress of Life,* Hans Selye lays down a basic principle: "The great lesson is to realize the deep-rooted biologic necessity for completion." Man must evolve something out of the chaos of his environment that he can call his own. His hands must mold and his mind generate changes in his environment, for only thus can he prove himself master of his fate and captain of his soul. But in spite of accusations against our economic system, the so-called establishment and the business world—attacks so vigorously and sincerely pursued by those who would right the many wrongs—it still remains a consideration that, according to Robert Waelder, in *Basic Theory of Psychoanalysis,* ". . . selfishness, greed, and destructiveness are part of the human makeup, and the economic system of competitive enterprise, far from creating them, merely channelizes them." Although many would question this point of view, it may be true that aggression thus directed is at worst far less noxious than the outlets they would otherwise find, and at best highly useful. This argument seems to indicate that one can certainly engage in capitalistic competition without selling his soul in the process.

But self-expression may be hindered by fears and doubts. To the faint-hearted many things are threatening, and the tendency to withdraw is encouraged by a multitude of fears that frustrate the very core of himself. All behavior may be placed in one of three categories: one either moves toward an object, or moves away from it —or remains fixed and unmoving. One confronts a problem, runs away from it, or does nothing about it. Fear will cause a person either to shy away from obstacles in his path or to accept defeat without a struggle.

The need to be comparatively free from fears is therefore one that must be met if this source of severe frustration is to be lessened, if one's powers to move forward are to be reasonably restored.

Some people are afraid of some vague and possible disaster, are afraid of other people perhaps because they may be members of a minority economic, social, religious, or national group. They may express fear of God and of the devil—always running away from these many fears and others, hiding within themselves the ghosts of their neurotic anxieties, perhaps daydreaming, worrying about what might happen. They are the defeatists rather than the activists.

A child is born with only two basic fears, the fear of loud sounds and that of falling. All other fears are learned. Someone, something has taught us how to be afraid of so many things. But anything learned can be unlearned.

Our fears must be attacked ruthlessly, with all the hatred we are capable of, flinging our hostility upon them, challenging them, slashing them with our understanding if possible, but always to attack and attack again. Our days of retreat are over. Our fears must be confronted boldly, exposing them for all to see. We shall desensitize every one of our fears, talk about them with anyone who will listen, meet them eye to eye, laugh at our phobias, and the monstrosities that hid so long within us will be dragged out because at last we have decided to be free. On this day we have taken our stand, and armored with hate we shall strike out, now the master of our destiny because we have willed to use hostility as a tool against the weaknesses inherent in past cowardice. It matters not the cause of fears; what does matter is that in deciding to fight, we have challenged them either to destroy us entirely or we shall slay them with awful vengeance and resolution. From then on we can never be the same; the times of passive acceptance are over, and from now on we dare to hate the negative as never before. We have joined the side of life, the side of the angels, spurned the death instinct as we suddenly realize what power resides in well-directed aggression to cleanse the human soul from its own treacherous alliance with the death instinct.

Our sense of guilt, another monster, must be similarly exorcised. The need to be free from guilt cries out to be met—and we are all to some degree prevented from self-realization by guilty feelings that have stunned and still continue to stifle our emotions from early childhood onward, either consciously or subconsciously influencing us toward inadequacy and weakness. We might note the Bible quotation (Rom. 14:14): "I know and am persuaded by the Lord Jesus that there is nothing unclean by itself, but to Him that esteemeth anything to be unclean, to Him it is unclean."

Guilt, of course, is the product of conscience, the ability to form moral judgment and to feel moral obligations. But what is the origin of conscience? Did we start life with a stock of moral judgments and moral feelings already present in mind, or did we have to acquire these through experience, their acquisition being a matter of our own gradual development morally?

The first view is called intuitionalism. It assumes that the first human being started life fully equipped with an inborn stock of moral judgment and moral feelings, and that every other human since then has started life in the same way. Our knowledge of right and wrong, therefore, is not an accumulation gained through experience but a native endowment implanted by heredity. This concept enables man to feel right and wrong as if he had an inner sense organ by which the rightness or wrongness of any particular act is immediately perceived.

Another point of view is dramatically opposed to the above assumption. This view, called empiricism, assumes that a man's moral judgments and moral feelings are not a native endowment, but the product of man's own experience. They are learned. Conscience develops through the influence of environment. Its formation has resulted from man's contact with man in social relationship.

The first approach, intuitionalism, is dictatorial; man must accept passively the dictates of his conscience, embracing his guilt as just punishment. The second, empiricism, allows the person to impose his will upon his conscience. If this conscience is merely the result of human experience, it is the dictates of others and therefore can be misleading and in fact exploitative. The door is open to freedom of choice. Man may challenge his conscience in the name of freedom and his own self-determination by changing his motives and experiences.

However, there are three senses in which the term freedom has been used. It sometimes denotes liberty or freedom from external restraints, as when a prisoner is set free from prison. This was the sense in which it was used by the Greek Stoics. According to this concept, no human being is considered free, for all are conditioned or restrained to a greater or lesser extent by the external environment.

Sometimes the term freedom is used to denote the ability to act from chosen motives. In this sense, every normal human being is free. In a third sense the term freedom refers to the power of alternative choice. However, when man makes a choice between two alternative courses of action, could he have chosen differently or was he obliged to choose as he did?

Just how free is man? To what extent is he capable of lessening his frustrations, and therefore lessening his anger?

One view, known as *determinism,* affirms that every man's career in life is determined by some power external to himself. Naturalistic fatalism places this power in the external world of nature, of which man is regarded as a mere mechanical part. This kind of fatalism is implied in "behaviorism." Supernatural fatalism places this power in some supreme being or beings. The story of Laius and Oedipus in Greek mythology illustrates the crasser form of supernaturalism. A much more refined form of supernatural fatalism is set forth in Augustine's doctrine of "predestination."

A view entirely and diametrically opposed to determinism is *indeterminism,* which assumes that man has the power of choice, that is, the power to act independently of motives altogether. Closely allied is the concept of *self-determination,* the idea that all choices are motivated by desires and goals set by man himself. This latter approach involves deliberation—the participation of man's intellect and the choice of strongest motives.

By assuming that man is a mere instrument of external factors, one denies his freedom. He becomes passive, a tool for the death instinct that favors inertia. On the other hand, when he confronts the fact that he is fully responsible for his own action, he places himself on the side of the positive and the life instinct. He must cease blaming powers other than himself or the traumatic experiences of his childhood as excuses for his timidity and lack of self-responsibility. His conscience may have been molded long ago by other influences, by unwise parents—and perhaps also by society itself as a means of making him a subservient citizen. The time comes, however, when the individual must stand on his own feet and grasp the control of his destiny in the here and now. Admitting that he is still influenced by subconscious tendencies, he can still face himself as he really is—working with what he has. He must stop bemoaning that others may be more fortunate than he, or that some childhood experiences must today dominate his behavior.

According to many psychologists, a person's needs can be met by assuming more responsibility. Mental illness always involves lack of responsibility, the refusal to take on one's own burden, the abrogation of one's own fate. Psychological disorders are created by refusing to assume responsibilities. Determining one's course of action is the road away from irresponsibility.

Throughout recorded history, men have been told that they have no right to live as they should determine, but must surrender their minds and bodies to emperors, kings, deities, priests, witch doctors, tribes, groups, and nation-states. Basic to that assumption was the belief that a person is inherently worthless, that he must be molded by self-appointed guardians and benefactors in order to be kept on the right track. Conceding, then, the knowledge of our weaknesses, we make use of our personal inadequacies merely as stepping-stones to a better life-style and a higher state of consciousness. Alfred Adler pointed out this basic principle by saying: "As normal sentiments the striving for superiority and the feeling of inferiority are naturally complementary; we should not strive to be superior and to succeed if we did not feel a certain lack in our present condition."

It is true that man is perhaps often wretched and revolting, petty and evil. Yet for all his misery, he is still the highest good. Sophocles said, "Wonders are many, and none is more wonderful than man." And he must dare to face himself, seek to understand himself. He must push that understanding as far as possible to others, to his community and finally to the world. Acting then boldly according to his own criteria, namely, his own welfare and that of others, he can be master of himself. In fact, the very permissiveness generated in our society proves a challenge when he is ready to release in the right way whatever hatred may thus be uncovered.

His course is clear; his scale of values definite: Is it good for me —and also for my fellowman? That is the ruler by which he measures his behavior. Of course, he will make mistakes. But if his motives have been good, guilt will not be his lot because he has acted according to what he deemed to be worthy causes.

First, then, he must take an inventory of his needs and determine which are not being met by asking the question, "What do I really want?" We have a right to determine our wants, no matter how foolish these may appear to others. The subsequent course of action taken to satisfy those needs will be good and justified if it improves the welfare of the person and at the same time the welfare of the group, the community, and the world. But one might counter, "How do I know whether I judge rightly my needs and those of my fellowmen?" The answer must be that you cannot relegate those responsibilities to others. Your decision, right or wrong, is your badge of courage by which you stand or fall. To be human is not to be perfect; one must dare to meet the consequences of poor decision and of an unwise course of action.

The procedure is to make up one's mind to act in what is presumed to be a forward direction, and then to call upon all our aggressive tendencies to propel us onward. The goal is to fulfill needs and desires. The motive power that takes us to that goal is our aggression. We fight for our self-realization as our ancestors fought their arduous environment and the enemies that lurked in the darkness. Two useful accomplishments are thus attained: our needs are met, providing us with a sense of well-being, of being alive and dynamic; and secondly a constructive outlet has been made available for our hostilities.

In the process we have learned to hate the cruelty and indifference of this world; we fight against the poverty. We detest ignorance and prejudices that make people suspicious of anyone who does not think like them, dress like them, talk as they do, go to the same church or club. Pity must not prevent us from confronting those who would rob us of our needs. Pity is frequently a facade hiding cowardice and indecision. A man and wife, for example, may remain together out of pity for one another or "for the sake of the children." It would perhaps be kinder to confront each other squarely, separating instead of living in bitterness and allowing it to spread upon all in the household.

In the course of improving ourselves, meeting our own needs while at the same time helping others, we have harnessed our hatred to the stars, stepped in harmony with universal designs, and had our powers augmented by the life instinct. Hatred has been effectively tapped for construction rather than destruction and in the process has been drained and purged, leaving man what he was meant to be, emancipated at last from inner turmoil.

It is only when man's hatreds are thus channeled away from himself that he becomes capable of love. Having released a demon from his soul, he opens his being to love and affection that hatred denied. He was then incapable of love as the hostility bred ever greater within him. But now that he has flung it against the environment for his welfare and that of his fellowmen, his being has both the time and the capacity to love and to receive love. His humanity has at last been given the opportunity to come through, no longer hindered by self-hate.

Mastery over hate comes when it has been expressed positively, when the instinctive energies that went into the formation of hate can be applied to purposes acceptable to the individual because it is productive both to him and the environment. This process strengthens the personality, increasing its capacity for tolerating frustration, and releasing it for constructive purposes. The destructive forces that hitherto beset the individual from within are thus harnessed to the best in him for self-realization and the betterment of mankind.

A dynamic person grasps fulfillment through action and confrontation. In a sense, he must find himself and extract concessions from the environment by becoming a doer, changing the surroundings closer to his heart's desire. The day has come when he refuses to allow hatred to poison his system because of the mistaken notion that it must remain there. Instead he will fling it against injustices and in that way replenish his body with righteous indignation to correct some of the wrongs that beset society. Meanwhile, the expression of any act of aggression serves as a catharsis that reduces the instigation to greater acts of aggression and thereby tends to reduce hatred.

On all sides, the acute problems of our day brood and stir. Anger must be shifted outward in a crusade for the betterment of the self and that of fellow human beings. Out of the hate that hitherto was so often exploited for vested interests, frequently erupting in criminality or exploding uncontrolled without guidance or purpose, that emotion must emerge with new aims and achievement.

What are these areas that cry for attention, where people bleed, too frequently silent with the numbness of great sorrow or deadening complacency? Where can I throw out the gauntlet of my hates? Where must I fight, no longer passive, always pressing forward in a will to improve my lot and that of my neighbors—and in the process also exalt my own soul? No man is born without the inherent power to help both himself and others.

Many problems cry out for our attention, are worthy of our aggression and even hatred. These are the deficiencies in our national life which are constantly drummed into our consciousness by newspapers, magazines, and other media. He who claims that modern society fails to offer sufficient challenge must inevitably be blind to reality. It must be concluded that he has become insensate to his environment and to the ever-present possibility that each in his way can improve the world about him and also save his sanity and his dreams.

By becoming part of a movement for the common good, by enlisting energy in helping to solve some of the problems in our society, your own psychological needs can also be met. A sense of sharing and belonging will emerge, a feeling of achievement, together with a greater understanding of the world, a kinship with others who engage in the same battle for emancipation and justice, a tendency to rid yourself of fears and guilts because your actions are just; and finally can come the grateful affection of those whose lot has been improved. You will thus be too preoccupied working and striving for your fellowmen to hate them—or to hate yourself.

There are two great obligations: duty toward one's fellowmen, and duty toward oneself, allowing you to embrace nature within yourself, to stop running away from these obligations, and to enjoy the life pulsing in you. Walter Kaufmann in his study of *Existentialism from Dostoevsky to Sartre* made a statement of particular significance to our point of view: ". . . when we say that man is responsible for himself, we do not mean that he is responsible only for his own individuality, but that he is responsible for all men."

And yet we are reminded by Karen Horney that "Our culture is pervaded by competition, not only in the business and political fields, but in social life, love life, marriage, and other fields as well." Just as we must accept anger as a tool for the expression and realization of the self, so competition must be received as a challenge to achieve, to pit our strength and determination against things and persons who would prevent the meeting of our psychological needs and those who are similarly denied in our society.

You must therefore associate yourself with a cause, a crusade, by becoming a positive force toward alleviating the problems of society. There must be a commitment, involvement toward goals. No longer must you stand aside and let the world go by, thus stagnating with ever-mounting hatred in your heart. No one can really tell you how environmental and social problems may be solved. The solutions must come from yourself, in your own way, as part of your aggressive tendencies. No one can tell you how specifically to meet your own needs. That is your responsibility, the task that is your God-given right to decide; and the degree to which you assume that responsibility, to that extent will self-respect and self-fulfillment be achieved.

The time is perhaps near when ordinary citizens can no longer be compelled helplessly to turn hatred against the self or against imagined foreign enemies. Aggression, and its close relative, hate, can instead be used to attack the evils of society, to mold the inner recesses of our souls, and to change the outer world nearer the desires and the innate rights of man in a free society—to evolve an environment where the individual can walk in dignity and self-respect, a positive being instead of a negative pawn subject to forces beyond his control.

Index

A

abandonment, by mother, 6-7
abortion, 5-6, 43
abstention, sexual, 48-49
adjustment mechanism, 15, 84, 96
aggression, 10-11, 54
  denial of, 66, 81
  expressing, 33, 59-60, 72, 99, 107
  harnessing, 22
  sexual, 38
  sublimation of, 19, 20, 45
alcohol, addiction to, 98, 100
anger
  as cause of frustration, 56
  constructive, 9, 33-34, 36, 54, 63, 74
  dealing with, 57, 62, 72
  destructive, 21-22, 63, 74
  expression of, 66-67, 101
  justifiable, 78-88
  nature of, 10-17, 25-32
  repression of, 18, 28, 58, 71, 90, 92, 101
  sexual, 45, 46, 48
automobile accidents, 88-100

B

behavior
  acceptable, 23
  aggressive, 18
  antisocial, 14, 26, 68, 93, 107
  uncontrollable violent, 99

C

capital punishment, 75-77
child abuse, 28-30
childhood, hurts of, 25-32
conflicts, racial, 83-84
conformity, need for, 36
criminality, and anger, 66-77
cult, religious, 41-42

D

death instinct, 107-108
delinquency, 37, 60
depression, 16, 26, 46, 48, 56-57, 65, 97
determinism, 115
dilation and curettage, 5
dropouts, school, 2
drugs, 81, 97
  addiction to, 22, 37, 100
  in schools, 2
dysfunction, sexual, 48

E

eating disorders, 25, 100
empiricism, 114-115
escapism, 37

F

family, decline of, 34, 79
fixation, developmental, 101-102
frustration, 2, 10-11, 13, 14, 15, 23, 37, 40, 54,
  67, 100, 109
  childhood, 25-32, 74
  and neurosis, 89-90
  of prison life, 70
  sexual, 17, 20, 46, 48, 100-101
frustration-aggressive hypothesis, 11, 19, 20,
  67, 70, 71

G

gang, adolescent, 68, 83
guilt, feelings of, 16, 19, 26, 31, 43, 45, 46,
  48, 67, 93, 99, 114, 117, 119

H

hair, societal meanings of, 38-39
handicap, dealing with, 88
hate
  car as outlet for, 82, 98-100
  constructive, 12, 18-24, 79, 118
  deflected, 12, 14-15, 20
  destructive, 45, 99, 107
  explosive, 12, 13-14, 19, 20, 58-65, 100
  incipient, 12-13
  inward, 12-13, 19, 57, 71, 81
  of mother, 6
  repressed, 58-59, 102
  self-, 90, 91, 93, 108, 118
  uncontrolled, 11-12, 53
heredity, 67-68
homosexuality, 4, 31, 43
hypocrisy, 25, 28, 41, 45, 106

I

incest, 47
independence, drive for, 40-41
indeterminism, 115
intuitionalism, 114-115

L

loneliness, 6, 80
love, 118
  imposed by society, 26

121